THE MYSTERIOUS ITALIAN HOUSEGUEST

BY

SCARLET WILSON

First published in Great Britain 2017
By Mills & Boon, an imprint of HarperCollins*Publishers*
1 London Bridge Street, London, SE1 9GF

Large Print edition 2017

ISBN: 978-0-263-07160-3

MIX
Paper from
responsible sources
FSC C007454

This book is produced from independently certified FSC paper to ensure responsible forest management. For more information visit www.harpercollins.co.uk/green.

Printed and bound in Great Britain
by CPI Group (UK) Ltd, Croydon, CR0 4YY

THE MYSTERIOUS ITALIAN HOUSEGUEST

CHAPTER ONE

PORTIA CLOSED THE door behind her and breathed out as the car puttered off into the distance. Finally, peace perfect peace.

Somewhere, on the other side of the house, she could hear the chirrup of birds. After three days of being constantly surrounded by people and chatter it was music to her ears.

She leaned back against the cool wall, tempted to just slide down it.

Her sister Miranda's wedding was over. She could stop smiling. She could stop fending off the intrusive questions from her sisters. Miranda had looked radiant, lost in the pink cloud of love and drifting off somewhere that seemed a million miles out of Portia's reach.

She was the oldest sister—wasn't she supposed to get married first?

The tightness that had gripped her chest since she'd got here eased just a little.

The last wedding guest had left. Miranda was off on her honeymoon, Posy had gone back to work, and Immi had returned to her job in the family business. Finally, Portia could have some quiet.

It wasn't that she didn't love her sisters. Of course she did. It was just that being around them was so…busy. They all talked at once, and over the top of each other. And what she really needed right now was a chance to take stock, to weigh up what to do next.

Her discarded mobile phone lay on one of the gilded tables in the large entrance hall almost mocking her.

L'Isola dei Fiori had patchy mobile coverage. Villa Rosa had an old phone line that didn't currently work, and no Internet.

She didn't need emails. She didn't need a phone signal.

The last conversation on the phone had turned her work life upside down.

'What have you brought us in the last four

weeks, Portia? The award ceremony was weeks ago. Your red carpet interviews are yesterday's news. You're supposed to be an investigative reporter. This is Hollywood. And at twenty-seven your time is almost up. Bring me a headline story in the next four weeks or you're history.'

She'd felt numb. Studying investigative journalism at university had been a dream come true. Finding a job in Fleet Street had been much harder. When she'd decided to hitch around the US with a friend for a few weeks she'd no idea how her life would turn out. One random conversation in a small café in Los Angeles had led to a temporary job at a TV station as a runner. When one of the producers had found out what she'd studied he'd asked her to pull some material together for their entertainment gossip show. Portia was smart and Portia was beautiful. Two months later she'd still been there and when the TV host had been involved in an auto accident on the way to the studio, she'd filled in with less than an hour's notice. The audience had loved her. Social media had exploded. The gorgeous brunette with tumbling curls, dark eyes, plummy

English accent and sense of humour had attracted more viewers. Within a year the show had been a hit. All for a job that Portia had landed due to a complete fluke.

Five years on she'd broken more Hollywood stories than any of her rivals. The truth was, she'd been a little ruthless at first. She'd had a natural tendency to sniff out a story at fifty paces and her boss had quickly pushed her for more and more headlines. At first, she'd enjoyed it. She'd interviewed film stars past and present with aplomb. And while she'd charmed them with her smile, she hadn't lost her investigative edge. For the last five years she'd happily exposed liars, cheats and corruption in Hollywood. But as time had marched on the colours around her had muted a little. She was becoming jaded. She'd lost the fire that had once burned in her belly. Hollywood seemed to be a cycle, with only the faces changing while the stories sounded the same. And her boss was pushing and pushing her for more scandal-led headlines—the kind that had started to make her stomach flip over.

The thing was, she did have two major stories

she could break. But the conscience she'd developed wouldn't let her. One, about an elderly well-respected actor who was gay. As far as she was aware, virtually no one knew. And no matter how much the information spun around in her brain—and even though she knew it would make headlines around the world—she really didn't feel the urge to 'out' him. The second story, about a major actress who was secretly crippled by depression, would also make headlines. This woman was known for her sense of humour and smile. But it was all completely fake. The thing was, Portia knew why. Her daughter was very sick. And it was a story that she didn't think she should break either.

It played on her mind. Unless she could find another story in the next few weeks she would have to find a whole new career. And what kind of story could she find on L'Isola dei Fiori? A place with a tiny population and barely any mobile phone signal.

It might be time to take another look at that book she'd been writing for the last three years. Anything would be better than feeling like this.

A gentle sea breeze blew through the hallway. The back French doors must be open.

Space. That was one of the marvels of this place.

Portia wandered through to her favourite room of the house. The ceiling curved into a dome and the washes of blue, mauve and pink—even though faded—made it seem as though a magical sunset were taking place right above your head. If she closed her eyes she could remember this house in its prime. It had belonged to Sofia, her sister Posy's godmother. Sofia had been a famous model and, a number of years ago, the then Prince's mistress. If Portia could turn back the clock she'd love to interview Sofia. When she was a child it had all just seemed so normal. A godmother who lived in a huge house on a mystery island, sweeping up and down the grand staircase in a whole array of glittering gowns like some forgotten starlet.

If she closed her eyes she could remember most of the movie stars, rock stars and models of the nineties that had filled the rooms in this house. If she could really turn back the clock she would pay more attention to some of the conversations and liaisons she could vaguely remember hearing and witnessing.

Coming to L'Isola dei Fiori had always been such an adventure. The flight to Italy and then the journey over on the ferry had always seemed like part of a children's story complete with the image of the pale pink Villa Rosa sitting on the headland.

But Villa Rosa wasn't quite as magnificent as it had remained in her head. The pale pink stucco had cracked and faded. The exotic flowers in the gardens had been surrounded by weeds. Part of the scullery roof had fallen in and been mended by Miranda's new husband, Cleve, along with some of the ancient electrics in the house. It seemed that in years gone by each room had only required one plug point.

Portia ran her hand along the wall. Some of the plaster was crumbling. There was a crack running up the wall towards the top of the dome, bisecting part of the beautiful paintwork. The whole place was more than tired. Parts of it were downright neglected.

Even though Posy had inherited it from Sofia, all the sisters felt an element of responsibility. They'd all enjoyed holidays here as children. Sofia had been the ultimate hostess. Sipping cocktails and treating the girls like adults instead of children. There had been no fixed bedtimes. No explicit rules. As long as the girls were respectful and well-mannered Sofia had seemed to be entirely happy.

Villa Rosa conjured up memories of lazy days with beautiful sunrises and sunsets, long hours on the private beach and by the hot spring pool, the many legends about the craggy rock arch bisecting the beach, and a flurry of fun in a rainbow of satins, silks and sequins. Sofia had had the most spectacular designer wardrobe and she hadn't hesitated to let her mini charges play dress up.

Portia leaned against the wall and sighed. The ugly crack annoyed her. Doubtless it would require some specialist to repair it. Like most of this house. Why did it feel as if the house was reflecting her life right now?

She couldn't remember. Was Villa Rosa a listed

building? Did they have listed buildings in L'Isola dei Fiori? Miranda and Cleve had done some emergency repairs on the house. There were a few liveable rooms. But the kitchen and bathrooms were antiquated and barely functioning. The dusty full attics would probably be an antique dealer's dream. But Portia knew nothing about things like that and was too wary to even attempt to help with a clean-up for fear she would throw something valuable away.

She breathed in deeply. The warm sea air was wafting through the house bringing with it the aroma of calla lilies, jasmine and a tang of citrus from the few trees along the wall of the garden. She sighed, walked through to the kitchen and retrieved a semi-chilled bottle of rosé wine from the sometimes functioning fridge, grabbing a glass and walking through the double doors to the glass-ceilinged conservatory. There was a sad air about it. A few of the delicate panes were missing or cracked. At some point Sofia had commissioned a specialist stained-glass maker to install some coloured panes in a whole variety of shades, randomly dotted throughout the conservatory. It meant that when the sun streamed in from a particular angle the conservatory was lit up like a rainbow, sending streams of colour dazzling around the space. The doors at the end of the conservatory opened out to the terrace and gardens, which led to the sheltered cove below with a bubbling hot spring. It really was like a little piece of paradise.

She settled on an old pale pink wooden rocker sitting on the terrace that creaked as she sat down. She smiled, holding her breath for a few seconds for fear the wood might split. But the rocker held as she poured her wine then rested her feet on the ledge in front.

The azure sea sparkled in front of her. The horizon completely and utterly empty. It was as if the whole rolling ocean had been made entirely for her viewing pleasure.

She closed her eyes for a second. There was something about this place. Something magical.

In her head she could see the glittering parties that Sofia had hosted. Full of film stars, models, producers, and Sofia's very own special Prince. Portia sipped her rosé wine, letting the dry fresh flavour with hints of cherry and orange zest fill her senses as she rocked back and forward in the chair.

If she could capture just one of those moments, and bring all the gossip twenty years into the future, she wouldn't need to worry about her job any more. Times had been different then. No instant social media. No mobile phones in every pocket or every bag.

She gave a little smile as she closed her eyes and continued to rock. A warm breeze swept over her, scented with jasmine and hugging around her like a comforting blanket. It was almost as if time had stood still at Villa Rosa.

And for Portia's purposes, that was just fine.

Javier finished nursing his last bottle of beer. He'd crossed over on the last evening ferry to L'Isola dei Fiori and, instead of heading straight to the house, he'd headed straight to the nearest bar.

L'Isola dei Fiori had been a favourite haunt of his mother's. Her friend Sofia's house had been a refuge for her when her manic behaviour had got out of control, she'd stopped eating and stopped taking her medication. His father had learned quickly not to try and intervene. Sofia's presence had been one of calmness and serenity. A fellow model, she'd understood the ingrained eating habits and learned behaviour that his mother just couldn't shake in later life. Even though she was always beautiful in Javier's eyes, as his mother had aged she hadn't taken kindly to losing modelling jobs. Each loss had seemed to spark more erratic behaviour and his film producer father had struggled to cope.

Javier had been too young to understand much. He'd just learned that when his father pulled out the large monogrammed case, it generally meant a visit to Aunt Sofia's. She'd never really been an aunt, but he'd thought of her in that way. Sofia's air of grace could never be forgotten. She hadn't walked—she'd glided. She'd talked to him as if he were an adult, not a child, with no imposed rules or regulations. Instead, Javier had been mainly allowed to amuse himself. Not always wise for a young boy.

But somewhere, in the back of his brain, he'd

held fast the little element that this place was a sanctuary. Somewhere to find calmness. Somewhere to find peace. And that was what he needed right now. A place where the paparazzi weren't waiting around every corner. A place where he could nod at someone in the street without their frowning and wondering where they'd seen him before. A place where he could have a drink in a bar without someone whipping out their phone to take a selfie with him in the background.

He left his money on the bar and picked up his bag. He'd been here for at least three hours with minimal conversation. He liked that. The hours of travel had caught up with him. He patted the large iron key in his pocket. At some point over the years his mother had 'acquired' a key to Villa Rosa. It was odd. Neither of them had been back since Sofia's funeral a few years ago and he'd heard that the house, once in its prime, was now pretty run-down.

Maybe he could make himself useful while he kept his head below the parapet for a while. When he was a teenager his Uncle Vinnie—a veritable handyman—had taken him on many of his jobs. Anything to keep him from turning down the wrong track. At the age of thirteen, with a mother as a model and a father as a film producer, he'd probably already seen and heard a million things he shouldn't. After he'd almost dabbled with some drugs, his father had shipped him back to Italy and into his brother's care for the summer. Javier had learned how to plaster and how to glaze. It appeared that sanding and smoothing walls, and cutting panes of glass were therapeutic for a teenage boy. Not that he'd used any of those skills in Hollywood…

He walked out into the warm evening. Dusk was settling around him. The port was still busy with the boats silhouetted against a purple and blue darkening sky. If he were an artist he would be tempted to settle down with some paints, a canvas and easel. But Javier Russo had never been known for his painting skills.

Instead, his name normally adorned the front of Hollywood cinemas. His latest film had just been publicised by putting a forty-five-foot-high image of Javier next to the *D* on the Hollywood sign. He'd never live that one down.

But it seemed that Hollywood loved Italian film stars. In another year it was predicted he'd be one of Hollywood's highest earners—much to his agent's delight.

He'd just finished four back-to-back movies taking him halfway around the world. Two action movies, one romantic comedy and one sci-fi. He'd ping-ponged between the Arabian Desert, the expanse of the Indian Ocean, the nearby island of Santorini, the Canadian Rockies and the streets of London. For some it sounded completely glamorous. In truth it was lonely and had taken him away from those that he loved. The family that he'd failed.

Now, he was exhausted. Pictures had emerged of him attending the funeral of a family friend looking tanned and muscular—just as well nothing could reveal how he was feeling, the way his insides had been curling and dying from the fact he hadn't been there to help.

Much to his agent's disgust he'd reneged on some immediate future arrangements. In another four weeks the cycle would start again with publicity and interviews for the first of those films. Right now he needed some space.

He smiled as he turned the corner to Villa Rosa. The long walk had done him some good. He stretched muscles that had been cramped on the flight over from Los Angeles and frowned at the cracks in a pale pink façade. This place was in bad need of repair. He wasn't entirely sure about the material. Maybe he could phone Uncle Vinnie for some advice?

He set his bag down and pulled the key from his pocket. With a wiggle, the key gave a satisfying turn in the lock. He pushed the door open not quite knowing what to expect.

Silence.

He frowned. Something was off. The house wasn't as musty as he'd expected. He walked slowly through the large main hall. It was clear someone must have been here. There were small signs of life.

Large dust covers had been pulled from the furniture in the painted room and heaped in one corner. He ran his finger along the plaster, snatching it back as a tiny piece of paint flaked to the ground. In the dim light his eyes caught the line snaking up the curve of the dome. He felt his frown deepen. It would take skill to mend a crack like that. Skill he wasn't sure he possessed.

He glanced around him. The air in here was fresh. There was a hint of something else. The rustling from outside sounded far too close. Windows were open in this house.

He strode through towards the back of the house. The conservatory had seen better days. A few of the small panels of glass were missing and others were cracked or damaged. Something crunched beneath his feet. He knelt down; a small fragment of red glass was under his shoe. He brushed it off as he heard a small cough.

His head shot back up, looking out across the terrace.

A woman.

Who on earth was here?

According to his mother this place had been deserted since Sofia had died. That was why it had fallen into the state it was in. He hadn't stood up yet. Wondering how to deal with the mysterious woman on the terrace.

Could she have broken in? Was she some tourist who had spotted the giant pale pink neglected house and decided she could squat here? He moved his head, squinting at the figure.

A brunette. In her twenties. Dressed in something short and red. He shifted uncomfortably. Whatever she was wearing, it seemed to have inched upwards as she lay in the rocking chair, sleeping with her legs stretched out and resting on the low wall. He could see a hint of black underneath. She moaned a little and shuffled in her seat, the hard wood beneath her obviously not as comfortable as she wanted. The chair rocked back and forth.

He straightened up, trying to get a better look. On the terrace was an empty glass and a bottle of wine. Was she drunk?

Maybe Sofia had a wine cellar that everyone had forgotten about and some light-fingered thief was now drinking her way through the contents?

Now, he was getting angry. He'd come here for some peace. Some tranquillity. The last thing he wanted was to have to call out the local *polizia*.

He strode out onto the terrace ready to tackle

the intruder. But his footsteps faltered. He'd only really glimpsed her from sideways. Now he could see her clearly he was surprised.

Her hair tumbled around her face, chocolate at the roots, blonde-tipped courtesy of the sun—or a salon. Her dress was indeed almost around her hips revealing her well-shaped firm legs blessed with a light golden tan. Her chest went up and down lightly beneath the thin cotton of her dress that did little to hide her curves.

There was something vaguely familiar about her. Something he couldn't quite place.

His foot crunched on a stone on the terrace and her eyes flew open.

Before he even had a chance to speak she was on her feet, her eyes wide and her hands grabbing for the nearest item.

'Mi scusi, non volevo spaventarti...'

He'd automatically reverted to his native language but it did nothing to stop the wine glass being hurled in his direction and catching him squarely on his brow. It shattered at his feet on the terrace as he took another step towards her.

This time she had the wine bottle, brandishing it like a weapon in front of her.

'Don't move, buster. Take another step and I'll…I'll…'

She glanced sideways. And he caught the wave of fear that had rolled over her.

But the comedy of the moment hadn't escaped him. He stepped forward and took the empty wine bottle firmly from her hands and smiled. 'You'll spring vault backwards past the hot spring and straight down to the beach and the lovers' arch?'

Her eyes widened even further. If it were possible they were the biggest brown eyes he'd ever seen. Like a dark whirlpool that could suck you right in.

Waves of confusion were sweeping over her face. The obvious change from Italian to English seemed to have caught her unawares. Her head flicked sideways to the lovers' arch. He could almost read her mind. Only someone who was familiar with this property would know about the hot spring and private beach beneath.

And there was still something vaguely familiar about her…

Her body was still stuck in the vaguely defensive stance. 'You know about Neptune's arch?'

The accent. That was what it was. And those eyes. The plummy accent had sounded strange when she'd shouted so quickly. A bit like a member of the British royal family yelling at him. He smiled again and set the bottle down on the terrace, folding his arms across his chest.

He was around ten inches taller than her. He didn't want to intimidate her. She didn't look like the cat-burglar type.

He let out a laugh. 'I invented it.' Then shook his head, curiosity piqued even further. 'I didn't tell you it was called Neptune's arch.'

She jerked. As if she were getting used to his Italian accent speaking English to her.

Her gaze narrowed. Now, she looked angry. She planted her hands on her hips. 'Who on earth are you, and what are you doing in my house?'

'Your house?' He raised his eyebrows. 'Are you Sofia's goddaughter?'

She shook her head. 'Yes. Well…no.'

'Well, make up your mind. You either are, or you aren't.'

She gritted her teeth. 'No. Posy is Sofia's goddaughter. She's my sister.' She frowned again. 'But who are you? And how do you know Sofia?'

The more she spoke, the more he felt the waves of familiarity sweeping across his skin. She wasn't an actress. He knew every British actress that spoke as she did.

The hairs on his arms stood on end in the cool coastal breeze. Realisation was hitting home. Chances were this English siren was staying here. All hopes of hiding away on this island in peace and quiet were gently floating away in the orange-scented air.

'Sofia was a good friend of my mother's. We stayed here often when I was a child and a teenager.'

She mirrored his position and folded her arms across her chest. 'Well, you're not a teenager now and Sofia's been dead for two years.'

'I was at her funeral. I never noticed you.' Even as he said the words he was struck by the realisation that he wasn't likely to forget a woman like this. She was downright beautiful. As beautiful as any one of his Hollywood leading ladies.

In fact, she was much more natural than most of them. No Botox. No obvious surgery. And skin that was clear and unblemished. If only the public knew just how much airbrushing went on in film studios.

It made him smile that she didn't remember him. Didn't recognise him.

But right as that thought crowded his brain, he saw the little flicker behind her eyes.

'What's your name? Who is your mother?' It wasn't a question, it was a demand.

Something sparked inside him. It had been a long time since someone had spoken to him like that. Being a Hollywood movie star meant he was usually surrounded by 'yes' people. Part of the point of coming here was to get away from all that. He just hadn't expected to reach the opposite end of the spectrum.

He sucked in a breath. 'You tell me yours, I'll tell you mine.'

Her beautiful face was marred by a deeper frown. He could sense she wasn't used to being lost for words. She drew herself up to her full height. She had bare feet and the top of her head was just above his shoulder. The perfect height for a leading woman.

'I'm Portia. Portia Marlowe.' She tossed her hair over her shoulder, glancing over at the azure sea, then rapidly sucked in a breath and spun around to face him as the recognition struck.

She pointed her finger. 'You're Javier Russo.' Her voice had gone up in pitch.

There it was. Anonymity gone in a flash. He sighed and walked over to the edge of the terrace. The beach looked inviting, even if it was a bit of a scramble to reach it. As a child he hadn't given it a moment's thought.

He almost laughed out loud at the thought of the film insurers' opinion on him staying in such a place. They'd want to wrap him in cotton wool. What on earth had his last action movie insured his legs for—ten million dollars?

The sun was dipping lower in the sky, sending dark orange streaks across the water. It was a beautiful sunset. He understood why she was sitting out there. But he still didn't know what she was really doing here. More importantly, was she staying?

She moved next to him. 'You're Javier Russo,' she repeated. Her voice was getting quicker. 'Javier Russo. Italian movie star.' She gave him a sideways glance. 'Thirty. Just finished filming a sci-fi film in the Arabian Desert, and last year the second highest paid action movie star.'

The hairs prickled at the back of his neck. He'd met hundreds of fans over the last few years. Some verging on the slightly obsessive. But he couldn't imagine he'd be so unlucky to end up staying with one of them on L'Isola dei Fiori.

'How on earth do you know that?' Something else flashed into his brain and he gave a half-smile. 'And what's with the look you gave me when you said I was thirty?'

'Is that your real age or your Hollywood age?' she shot back cheekily.

She waved her hand. 'Oh, come on, you know. Most Hollywood stars take a few years off their age. Some even more than ten.' There was the hint of a teasing smile on her face. She seemed to have regained her composure. 'But once you get up close and personal, you always know if it's an extension of the truth or not.'

He laughed out loud and turned back from the view to meet her head-on. There was a sparkle in her eyes. She'd obviously moved from the initial fear factor to the having-fun factor. She wasn't flirting. That didn't seem like her agenda. But she certainly seemed much more comfortable around him. And she wasn't tugging at her dress or hair. Often, once people recognised him, they frantically tried to get a glimpse of their own appearance, sometimes cursing out loud that they didn't look their best.

Portia didn't seem to care. Her simple red dress—which looked as if it came from any high-street store—stopped mid-thigh. The only remnant of make-up on her face was a hint of red stain on her lips.

He moved a little closer. 'So, what do you think?'

His chest was only a few inches from her nose. She looked a little surprised. She lifted her hand up and he wondered if she was going to push him away.

Her hand stayed in mid-air. 'Think about what?' Her voice had quietened and as she looked up at him the sun was in her eyes, making her squint a little.

It was as if a wall of silence fell around him. He was in a movie now. A glass panel had just slid around the two of them and cut out all the surrounding noise. No lapping waves. No breeze. No rustling leaves or tweeting birds.

All that was present was a girl in a red dress, with tiny freckles across the bridge of her nose and dark chocolate eyes. It was that tiny moment in time. A millisecond, when something reached into his chest and punched him square in the heart.

He'd met dozens of beautiful women. He'd dated some of them. Had relationships with others. But he'd never felt the wow factor. That single moment when…zing.

And he couldn't fathom what had just happened. It was that single look. That single connection.

She licked her lips.

And the sci-fi glass portal disappeared, amplifying all the noise around him. He swayed a little.

'Do I think that you're really thirty?' She threw back her head and laughed. 'Well, if you are—you're the only film star who doesn't lie about their age.' She lifted one hand. 'And don't get me started on their diets, workout plans or relationships.'

The wind caught her dress, blowing it against her curves. He took a step backwards.

'How do you know all this stuff?' His curiosity was definitely piqued. He'd heard that Sofia had a goddaughter. But he didn't know anything about her—or the fact she had sisters. Now, this sister—Portia—seemed weirdly knowing about Hollywood's poorly kept secrets.

'Do you work in Hollywood? How come I've never met you?'

Something glanced across her face. Hurt?

'I have met you,' she answered quietly.

'Where?' He tried to rack his brains. Somehow if he'd met her before he assumed he'd remember.

Her tone had changed. He'd definitely annoyed her. 'I met you at the award ceremony. I interviewed you on the red carpet about the pirate movie.'

She didn't even call it by its name—even though it had made one and a half billion dollars at the box office and counting.

The award ceremony—the biggest in Hollywood. That had been March. And reporters had lined the red carpet in their hundreds all hoping for a sound bite from a film star. Trying to remember anyone in amongst that rabble would be nigh on impossible.

It was as if someone had just dumped the biggest bucket of ice in the world over his head. He stepped back. 'You work for a newspaper?'

A reporter. Just what he needed.

The plague of the earth. At least that was what his mother used to call them. They'd harassed her to death when she'd been unwell. He had clear childhood memories of their home in Italy surrounded by people holding cameras and brandishing microphones, while his mother wept in her bedroom.

He'd learned early on to tell them nothing. Not a tiny little thing. Anything that was said could be twisted and turned into a headline full of lies the next day. Nothing had affected his mother's moods more than the press.

As a Hollywood star he couldn't possibly avoid them. But he could manage them.

And he always had. Two-minute press junkets. Any longer interviews done in writing by his press officer, along with a legal declaration about misquotes.

All press were to be kept at a distance. Even the pretty ones.

No, *especially* the pretty ones.

Her eyes narrowed a little. 'No, I work for Entertainment Buzz TV. Have done for the last five years.' She held up her hand and counted off on her fingers. 'I interviewed you after your first appearance in the Slattery action movies. I've met you at probably half a dozen film premieres and I met you on the red carpet in March.'

He was surprised she was offended. Every TV reporter in the world knew what press junkets were like. Each person was given an allotted time frame—usually around two minutes—along with a long list of questions they weren't allowed to ask. It was like speed dating—usually with a really boring outcome, because all the questions that were asked you'd already answered sixty times before.

He felt himself bristle. A reporter. Absolutely the last person he wanted to be around right now. Not when he wanted some privacy and some head space.

'Are you staying here?' He couldn't help the pointed way his words came out.

She blinked at the change of conversation and stuck her hands on her hips. The sea air swept across them both echoing the instant chill that had developed. 'It's my sister Posy's house. Where else would I be staying?'

'But this place is supposed to be deserted.' Frustration was building in his chest. He turned around and gestured at the fading building behind him. 'I mean, look at it. How long has your sister had it? She hasn't done any work at all. This place is falling apart at the seams.'

Portia's dark eyes gleamed. 'I think you'll find

that this place has been like this for around the last fifteen years. When was the last time you were here, *exactly*? Sofia let things fall by the wayside. She didn't keep up the house maintenance. After her relationship with Crown Price Ludano ended, I'm not sure she had the means.'

Portia glared at him. 'My other sister Miranda and her husband Cleve have made some temporary repairs to the roof and electrics. I was hoping to tidy up a bit while I was here. Posy is a ballerina. She doesn't have any spare funds right now, let alone enough money to carry out the extensive repairs that this place will need.' It was obvious she was on the defensive.

But so was he.

'Last I heard no one was staying here at all.' All the hairs on the back of his neck were standing on the offensive. Press. He had to get rid of her. How on earth could he sort things out with someone like her around?

'So you thought you would just break in?' she shot back.

He pulled the ancient large key from his pocket.

'I didn't break in. My mother has a key to Villa Rosa—she has done for years.'

'And that gives you the right to just appear here and let yourself in? My sister inherited this property. It's hers.' She placed her hand on her chest and raised her eyebrows. 'I know that I'm supposed to be here. But I'm quite sure you haven't asked her permission. Particularly when you don't even know her name.'

Javier was stunned. He wasn't used to people treating him like an unwanted guest. He certainly hadn't expected anyone to be here. He'd wanted the place to himself. But it was clear that wasn't going to happen.

It was too late now to go anywhere else. The last ferry to the mainland had left hours ago. There weren't any hotels nearby.

If Ms Portia Marlowe wanted to toss him out to the kerb, movie star or not, he was in trouble.

It was time to use the old Italian charm. He'd won awards for his acting. He might not mean a single word of it, but that didn't matter right now. He needed a bed for the night and could sort the rest of this out in the morning.

He smiled. He already suspected she might have had a few drinks. Maybe it was time to play on the situation.

He put his hand to his forehead and gave it a rub, throwing in a little sway for good measure. He wasn't an actor for nothing. 'Yeow!' He squeezed his eyes shut, then opened them, giving his head a shake.

She frowned. 'What's wrong?'

He gestured to the glass on the terrace. 'I didn't notice at first. But that glass packed a bit of a punch.' He shot her a smile and shook his head again. 'I'm fine. Just dizzy for a second.'

For the briefest moment her eyes narrowed, almost as if she suspected she was being played. But then, guilt must have swamped her. She moved forward and pointed towards the rocking chair behind them. 'Do you want to sit down? Will I get you some water?'

He gave a nod, and stepped backwards to the chair. It creaked as he lowered himself into the wooden frame and he prayed it wouldn't splinter and send him sprawling on the ground.

Peaceful quiet surrounded him.

From up here he could hear the lapping sea. Hear the rustling leaves. Hear the occasional chirrup of a bird. Tranquillity. This was what he'd come here for. This was what he'd hoped to find.

Aldo would have loved this place. He wished he'd had the chance to bring him. He would have adored the waves crashing into the cove. At one point Aldo had fancied himself as a surfer, but the sea had had other ideas. When they were young guys, every holiday Aldo had hired a surfboard and spent hour after hour wiping out. Most of the time they'd nearly drowned laughing. His fists clenched. Why had he never taken the opportunity to bring him to Sofia's? It spun around in his head, adding to the list of things he 'should' have done. Instead, time had just slipped away. Life had been too busy. There was always tomorrow.

Until there wasn't.

A fact he was going to have to learn to live with.

Too busy. Too busy filming. Too busy in meetings. Too busy to answer the phone to an old friend. He'd meant to call back that night. But after sixteen hours on set it had just slipped from his mind.

The next call he'd received had ripped his heart out.

That was why he'd come here. To find space. To find peace. For a reality check on the life he was living.

Instead, he'd found Portia Marlowe. A beautiful woman, but a Hollywood reporter. It was like a romance and a horror movie both at once. He would have to manage this situation carefully.

He closed his eyes and let the chair rock back and forth. Maybe she was due to go home in the next day or so? This might actually be okay. He only planned to stay here for a few weeks. Just enough time to give him some space. Some *alone* space.

There was a tinkling noise. Portia was on her knees sweeping the broken glass up with a dustpan and brush, her face a little pink. She caught his gaze and shrugged. 'I didn't know who you were. You caught me unawares.'

'So did you.'

The answer came out before he had time to

alter it. She looked surprised. Her dark gaze locked with his. Against the backdrop of the now purple and pink sky Portia almost looked as if she were standing inside the painted drawing room. A cameraman would wait hours for a shot like this. But right now, Javier was the only person with this view. Portia blinked, breaking their gaze and picking up the bottle of water she had next to her feet. 'Here, it's not too cold. The fridge seems to be a temperamental teenager right now. Sometimes it works. Sometimes it doesn't bother.'

He nodded and took the lukewarm bottle of water, his fingers brushing against hers. A film director would have added a little twinkle and sparkling stars to match the pulses that shot up his arm.

He pushed the feeling aside. Being attracted to Portia Marlowe wasn't an option. Not for a second. It couldn't go anywhere. He had enough to sort out without bringing a Hollywood reporter into the equation.

She leaned forward, the soft curves of her breasts only inches from his hand. Her thumb brushed his forehead. 'There's not even a mark. I should probably be relieved.' She gave a nervous laugh. 'Can you imagine the hoo-ha if I'd damaged the face of one of the world's most famous film stars?'

Her face paled and her hand gripped the edge of the rocker. His stomach sank. The enormity of her actions had just hit her—him too. A scar would have resulted in his agent and publicist probably having some kind of fit. In the space of a few seconds, he could see the headlines, the plastic-surgeon consultations, the juggling of schedules and the threatened lawsuits all from an action that hadn't really been intentional. It had been reactive. Not pre-planned. When he'd feigned feeling dizzy it had only been for his own ends. He didn't want to spend the night sleeping on the street when he'd come here uninvited. Now he felt like some kind of cad.

He breathed in slowly, inhaling some of her rose perfume. It was tantalising. Or maybe that was just Portia. He gave his head a quick shake, trying to realign his senses. 'I think maybe I just need to sleep. I've been travelling for a long time. I'm sure after a good night's sleep I'll feel fine.'

He let the words hang in the air. She opened her mouth to start to speak then closed it again. He could practically see the thoughts tumbling around in her brain. Her English sensibilities and good manners were obviously bubbling underneath the surface.

'I'm sure I can fix up a bed for you. One of the other bedrooms is almost cleaned. I did some laundry the other day.' There was hesitation in her voice.

Javier shot her his best smile. 'That's really kind of you. Thanks very much.'

He closed his eyes again as he heard her walk back into the house. He rocked back and forward in the chair. This was almost therapeutic.

And he needed that right now.

Because his time at Villa Rosa had just changed beyond all measure.

CHAPTER TWO

PORTIA LAY IN her bed wondering if the man in the next room was up yet.

Or maybe he'd died in the night of some hidden head injury she'd caused by throwing the wine glass?

She groaned and rolled onto her side. Sleep had been a stranger to her. She'd tossed and turned all night.

Somehow, Javier Russo had ended up sleeping in the room next to hers.

Talk about messing with her head.

She'd interviewed dozens of famous stars and met every personality trait. The smug. The bored. The sweetheart. The ignorant. The people pleaser. The desperate. And the person who appeared to be from another planet.

Javier had been charming in the way that only an Italian film star could be. But it was all an act.

Last time she'd met him he'd been arrogant. He could barely even bother to say hello. He'd looked at her with those steely grey eyes as she'd asked a question and replied, 'Is that really the best you can do?' before walking away with a dismissive glance. It was obvious he hadn't thought she'd been important enough to speak to.

Stars being rude was nothing new to Portia. But it had felt as though he was mocking her. And that had stung.

Most Hollywood stars at least pretended to like the press. Some tried to charm her. A few had even sent her gifts. One particularly sleazy older guy had slipped his hand a bit too low and earned himself a slap and he was *apparently* happily married. Five years in Hollywood had fast made her realise that everything was merely a façade. Hardly any of it was real—let alone the love stories.

The charm was all superficial. As for Javier Russo? Last time around he hadn't even feigned interest—she'd felt as welcome as something on the bottom of his shoe. It was only when his press officer had nudged him and whispered in his ear harshly that he'd tried to turn on the charm again—but with the next person in line.

And it had annoyed her beyond belief that as soon as he'd started to speak the rhythm of his words in that alluring tone had sent shivers down her spine.

That same voice that she'd heard last night.

She still wasn't entirely sure why he was there.

And that was pretty much the reason she couldn't sleep.

This was it. This was her chance. This was her chance for a story. Why on earth would Javier Russo be here? The man could probably afford to rent an entire hotel to himself. What on earth was he doing at Villa Rosa?

She tried to remember everything she'd ever heard about him. The truth was there was very little scandal around him. Yes, he was arrogant and sometimes aloof. But there were never on-set rumours about weird demands or keeping others waiting for hours. His star had definitely risen in the last few years and he'd been known to date a model, a pop star, and a few co-stars.

She hadn't realised his mother had been friends

with Sofia. They'd both been models around the same time; it made sense that they'd moved in the same circles. Sofia had photograph album after photograph album in the attic above Portia's head. Doubtless she would find some memento of the women's past history together.

In the meantime she was trying to keep calm. She shifted uncomfortably in the bed. This could be the story that could save her career. Or it could be nothing. It could simply be about a film star that had just filmed back-to-back movies and was looking for some peace and quiet. It wasn't really that outrageous a thought. Apart from an occasional interest in the royal family, L'Isola dei Fiori wasn't exactly the most sought-out destination. The ferry boat from the mainland was the only way here. Tourism was low. This place was off the beaten track. That was partly why she was here too.

But maybe it was something else? Maybe there was much more to Javier Russo than anyone knew. Her stomach flipped a little. She was still annoyed at him being so dismissive at their last meeting—one that he didn't even remember.

Maybe finding a story on Javier Russo would give her the boost she needed for her flagging career?

She pushed the horrible nagging feeling to the back of her head.

She'd only agreed to let him stay here one night. Maybe if there was a chance of a story she should reconsider?

There was a noise from downstairs. She frowned and swung her legs out of bed. It only took a few minutes to source where the noise was coming from.

Oh, Javier Russo was awake all right. He was so awake he was standing bare-chested in the painted drawing room. She rubbed her eyes. Maybe she hadn't woken up yet. Maybe this was all just some kind of weird dream. He was wearing a pair of blue jeans and black boots. And he was mixing something in a bucket, his actions allowing her to admire every chiselled muscle in his arms and abs. She was pretty sure her chin just bounced off the floor and came back up again. That smattering of dark curls across the chest then thickening and leading downwards… There should be a law against this kind of thing.

'What on earth are you doing?'

He looked up and smiled. 'Just making myself useful.'

There was quiet confidence in those words that actually made her smart. The painted room was her favourite in the whole house and she knew that Posy felt the same. Although they hadn't exactly spoken about it, she was sure that getting repairs done in a room like this was entirely outside all of her sisters' budgets.

He smeared some of the white plaster on a metal square he held in one hand. There were a number of different-sized trowels lined up on the floor, some brushes and a large open bag of plaster powder.

'Where on earth did you get all this?'

He smiled again. 'I borrowed the scooter parked in the garage and went to the local hardware store early this morning. If you know what you're looking for you can always find it.'

She shook her head as she eyed the bag of plaster. That had to be heavy. 'Where even is the hardware store? I didn't even know one existed.' She glanced at her watch. 'And when on earth did you go there?'

He shrugged. 'It's on the outskirts of Baia di Rose. Most tradesmen like to start their work early. They don't like to work in the heat of the day. The hardware store opened at six.'

He ran his hand along the wall and frowned, grabbing a piece of sandpaper and giving a gentle rub around the crack.

'What do you think you're doing? Don't touch that. You'll make it worse. This place is in a bad enough state without you deciding to play Mr Handyman.'

Javier sighed and shook his head. 'You act like I haven't done this before.'

'You haven't!'

He took a step closer and gave her a serious look. 'Don't you do your homework on the people you interview? I've said a number of times that I worked in the summers as a teenager with my Uncle Vinnie—the best handyman in the world.' He waved the piece of metal smeared with plaster. 'There are a number of jobs I can do around here in the next few weeks. Plastering was one of the things I was best at. I can repair the cracks and skim the walls in all the rooms. It will be a good foundation for any other decorating your sister has planned.' He waved his other hand. 'And the conservatory. I can replace the broken glass. Another of my specialities.'

Portia couldn't speak. She was astonished. She didn't like to be caught unawares. There were probably a million women the world over that would currently love to be in her position. A half-dressed Javier Russo offering to work as handy-man. She blinked and put her fingers at the edge of her hip and gave herself a sharp pinch.

Yep. She was definitely here. She was definitely awake.

He'd just criticised her. He'd implied she wasn't good at her job. He'd implied she didn't do her homework. Oh, this guy was clearly going to drive her crazy. Half naked or not.

And she hated to admit it right now, but she *didn't* know that much background on Javier Russo. Annoyance swept through her. She wasn't going to let him get the better of her. There was a story here. She could practically smell it in the air between them.

She licked her lips. Her intention had been to throw him out today. But the thought of a story was making her reconsider. Maybe she wouldn't mention anything today at all.

She glanced downwards and realised she was standing in her pale blue wrap robe and slippers, her hair tied in a tangled knot on her head. Not entirely appropriate. She'd been so focused on what the noise was she hadn't really thought about her appearance.

She sucked in a deep breath and tried to take a reality check on what was happening. She knew exactly how to play this. She laughed out loud and held up one hand, putting the other on her hip.

Javier looked amused. Perfect. 'What is it?'

She kept laughing. 'Well, I'm just thinking, whatever that wine was that I drank last night—and I only had two glasses—I think I better hunt down the rest of it.'

Javier lifted his hand from the wall. 'Why?'

She clicked her fingers. 'Well, look what's happened. I drink two glasses of wine, Javier Russo, world-famous movie star—and I think I remember you were last year's Most Eligible Bachelor—has turned up half naked in my sister's dilapidated old villa, offering to be my handyman for the next few weeks. This isn't real. There's no way this is real.'

He nodded slowly, contemplating her words. Javier had that tiny little gleam in his eye. It was famous. Often caught in pictures and on camera in films. It made him look as if he were talking to only you, sharing a joke only with you.

And right now, he *was* talking only to her. There was a real possibility of story here.

'What will it take to convince you?'

Her breathing stopped. Second time Javier Russo had caught her unawares. What did that mean? Her mouth couldn't find the next set of words.

For the tiniest second the thought of a story vanished. Instead, in its place, was the muscular body and grey eyes of Javier Russo. All man, right in front of her.

It was almost as if he read her mind. He put

the metal square on the floor next to the trowels and stepped closer. So close that his hand rested on her hip. Yes, it did. It really did.

If this were a film she would have spent around three hours in make-up achieving the 'natural' look. Unfortunately, her natural look was entirely natural. Her face scrubbed last night and a bit of her usual moisturiser smeared on her face. She always tied her hair up when she went to bed and it generally managed to tangle its way into an unruly mess.

He'd got close last night. But she'd gone from being a little foggy with the wine, to thinking there was an intruder, assaulting a movie star, then finding herself making up a bed for him.

No one would believe that interview.

All of a sudden she was closer than she'd ever expected to be with a movie star. Up close and personal. She could see every tiny line around his eyes. Laughter lines. No Botox. Every strand of his dark hair. The stubble on his jaw line. Her palm wanted to reach up and feel it. His white straight teeth and something hidden behind his grey eyes.

That was what stopped her in her tracks.

She recognised the signs. Hurt. Now she'd glimpsed it she could see it as clear as day.

He still hadn't told her why he was here. He hadn't answered many questions last night at all. Had he been dating? Was he here to mend his heart? Somehow, it didn't really seem to fit the bill.

Hurt. It confused her. What could hurt Mr Arrogant? The part of her conscience that had invaded her thoughts this morning crowded forward again.

She lifted both her hands and placed them on his bare chest. The heat against her palms sent tingles up her arms. It was completely forward. But it didn't feel that way. It felt natural. Honest. Her voice was barely a whisper. 'Javier, what are you running from?'

Beneath her palms his chest rose as he sucked in a breath. Silence. The TV host in her ached to fill it. More than three seconds of silence in front of the camera usually meant that something had gone wrong.

But her senses kicked in. The senses that were

still functioning while she had her hands on the chest of a film star.

He licked his lips and she stifled her groan. He was looking at her, but it didn't feel as if he were really *seeing* her. He was thinking about something else.

She watched as the virtual shields came down behind his eyes. The tiny part of Javier Russo she'd been about to see instantly hidden again. 'I've been busy. Four films in eighteen months and a whole range of press junkets for this year's new releases. I just needed a bit of time out.'

She bit her bottom lip. It was plausible. But it wasn't the truth.

'You have enough money at your disposal to go to a hundred private islands. You'd have as much peace and quiet as you want. Plus, you'd actually have a place with a functioning kitchen and bathrooms.'

He gave the hint of a smile and shook his head. 'But it wouldn't be the same.'

Something had changed behind his eyes. *Now*, he was being honest.

'What do you mean?'

He glanced down at her hands and her fingers jerked self-consciously. She should really move them. And she would. Just not yet.

He held up his arms. 'I mean, this is the place I remember. Once I got here as a kid, Sofia always filled it with happy memories. And I've never been a lie-on-the-beach kind of guy. I like to be doing something. I like to be industrious. It relaxes me. Helps me sort out things in my head. This place is my idea of a holiday. I just wish I'd thought of it a couple of years ago.'

Her stomach gave a little flip. Her head was all over the place right now. She'd planned to spend the next few weeks deciding what to do about her career. But she didn't really need to be here. She could be back in Hollywood right now, trying to dig up the career-defining story of a lifetime. Instead, she'd decided to take some time to contemplate her next step.

Entertainment Buzz TV had been good for her. She had a steady income. A nice apartment. A good lifestyle. She'd met more famous people—good and bad—than anyone could possibly want to. But things were changing. Hollywood had lost its glitter—even when there were men like Javier around.

Her mouth was dry. There could be a story right at her fingertips—literally. His arrogance had annoyed her before. But did she really want to dig deep and let him expose himself and his secrets to her? Was that really the type of person that she was?

'I want to stay here, Portia. Not in some hotel. Do you think that could be possible?'

Portia. He didn't say her name. He practically sang it.

He didn't even remember her. Not that she expected him to—really. But she had met him and interviewed him before. And it was kind of insulting for a guy not to remember you—even in cut-throat Hollywood.

Her rational head understood. At a press junket he met hundreds of journalists and could never be expected to remember them all. On award night he'd spoken to just as many again on the red carpet. She wasn't any different from any other person who'd shoved a microphone in his face and tried to think of an original question.

But it still stung.

And now he wanted to stay with her. Javier Russo wanted to stay with *her*.

She lifted her hands from his chest. She needed all her senses to be working. And they were already piqued. A fresh, clean scent drifted up under her nose. She scrunched up her face a second and tried to shake it off. The last thing she needed to think about was fresh, clean Javier Russo.

He'd lied to her. No, not strictly true. He just hadn't been entirely truthful. Why on earth would moneybags Mr Russo want to hide out in Aunt Sofia's home? He really wanted to get away from things?

It could be a story. But Internet was scarce around here, nearly as rare as a mobile phone signal. It was part of the reason she'd thought it was a good place to hide out.

She could get all defensive, like some creature marking out their territory, and tell him he couldn't stay. But…she could also be clever. There was always a chance she could get to the bottom of Javier Russo's story. It might just be the thing to save her career.

And in the meantime, she would have some company, and some eye candy.

She sucked in a breath and tried to find the ruthless streak she'd once had. 'You really just want to stay here?'

He nodded.

'How long for?'

Javier ran his fingers through his dark hair as he took a little step to the side. 'Not long. Just a few weeks.'

She folded her arms across her chest. 'You honestly just expected to show up, stay here and then leave, didn't you?'

His face creased into a smile. 'Well, kind of.'

She put her hand on her chest. 'And I've thrown a spanner in the works for you?'

He frowned for a second, as if he wasn't quite sure of the expression. But then he nodded. 'I get it.'

'You do?'

She stepped back a little, trying to get her head on straight for the first time since yesterday. Maybe it had been the wine. Maybe it had been the magical setting. But last night had been a bit unreal.

She gave him a serious look. 'Let's give this some perspective. Last night some stranger appeared at the place I'm staying. Okay, so he might have had a key—and a history of sorts with the place. But I'd made arrangements with my sister—' she put her fingers in the air '—the owner, to stay here for the next few weeks. I don't plan on going anywhere.' She pretended not to see the fleeting disappointment that shot through his eyes. 'We *both* thought we would have this place to ourselves.' She nodded out to the back conservatory. 'Let's face it. There's lots to be done here. And if you're as handy as you say you are, then I might not have any objections to you staying. My skills involve tidying up. That might sound mediocre, but, believe me, I've checked all the rooms and the attic—there's a *lot* of tidying up to be done.' She looked around the room as the acid in her stomach gave a little burn. She was trying her absolute best to be up front. She could hardly tell Javier that finding out what he was hiding from might save her career. Hopefully, it would be a woman. But that made the acid burn even more.

A picture of nails scraping down a chalkboard flashed into her brain with the associated noise. If it was trouble with a co-star, a contract, an affair—any of the above—it might just be enough to give her some leeway with her job.

It would save her telling the other secrets that weren't really hers to share.

She held out her hands. 'In the end, my sister needs this place to be liveable. If you can help with that, fine.' She shook her head and gave him a knowing glance. 'I just want you to know, I don't mix business with pleasure. Never have. Never will.'

Javier looked amused; the little glint was back in his eye. She liked it when that was there. It lightened the mood. She'd spent the last five years harmlessly flirting in front of the camera; it was the unwritten rule of TV hosts. She'd dated people in Hollywood. But never anyone to do with work. Dating a popstar/film star/TV star was the ultimate no-no. Inevitably there would be a messy fallout and he would tell all his fellow performers not to be interviewed by her. Two of her associated press members had found themselves almost blacklisted around Hollywood when their short-term flings had ended.

Portia was far too clever to be that girl.

Javier was watching her carefully. His tools were now on the floor and he made a grab for a T-shirt that she'd missed sitting on top of a white dust sheet.

'Come with me.'

'What?'

She followed him through the house to the kitchen, conscious of the fact she still didn't have on any real clothes. The kitchen—though ancient—was almost in working order. Miranda had arranged electricity and gas. Thankfully the water was still running. Portia had bleached a few cupboards in the last few days and put a few supplies away. But that didn't explain the bag on the countertop.

Javier pulled out some eggs and some freshly baked bread. 'I think our new arrangement calls for a celebratory breakfast.'

'We've made a new arrangement?'

He gave her his trademark Hollywood smile. 'Sure we have. I'm staying. I'll work on the plaster and arrange to get some glass for the conservatory.' He pulled out a frying pan and turned on the gas. 'How do you like your eggs?'

Portia sat up on a stool next to the countertop. 'You cook? And where did you get the eggs and the bread?'

'I got them when I went to get the supplies this morning.' He gave her a wink. 'I was a bit worried that the only sustenance in this place was wine.' He cracked the eggs as her cheeks flushed. But he hadn't finished. 'That was, of course…' he opened the cupboard nearest him '…until I found the candy supply.'

He was teasing her—she knew it. 'What can I say? There are fruit trees in the garden. Wine, fruit and chocolate. What more does a woman need?'

'What more indeed?' The sultry Italian voice shot straight through her, the suggestion in it taking her by surprise.

'Hurry up,' he said. 'Scrambled or fried?'

She stared into the pan. 'Fried is fine. Cooked all the way through.'

He narrowed his gaze. 'Yolk broken?'

'Don't you dare.' She sighed. 'I've never got the hang of sunny side up, over easy, over medium in the States and I've lived there five years now.'

'Maybe it's time to move back?' The hairs prickled at the back of her neck. Gossip spread fast in Hollywood. Did he know her job was on the line?

She tried not to sound as defensive as she felt. She had to remember that Javier could be the ticket to keeping her job. 'If I'm moving back, I'll need to hire a cruise ship to bring my clothes back. And my shoes. The studio doesn't let me keep any of the clothes I wear. But, due to the effects of social media, as soon as pictures start appearing the designers usually send me anything they've seen me wear—along with a whole host of other things. They like the publicity—' she shrugged as she broke off a piece of the bread '—and I like the clothes.'

He tossed the eggs. 'You took the job for the

clothes? I don't believe that. What did you do before you got the job?'

She walked over to the sink and filled up a pan with some water. She hadn't found a kettle, so the old-fashioned way would have to do. She set it on the gas hob next to where Javier was cooking. 'I studied investigative journalism at university. I was on holiday in the US, when I kind of lucked into the job. The rest—as they say—is history.' She gave his arm a nudge. 'A film star who makes his own food. Who would have thought it?'

He let out a laugh. 'What did you expect?'

She counted off on her fingers. 'Well, your last co-star on the action movie flew in his own personal chef, who ensured no meal was above three hundred calories. Your last female co-star was on that new-fangled diet where people only eat prawns and drink spring water.'

He rolled his eyes. 'No. You mean *chilled* spring water. We'll not talk about how the smell of prawns seemed to emanate from her pores.'

Portia laughed but kept going. 'Then, there was

the comedian in the sci-fi film who was on the spinach, Brussels sprout and fried beans diet.'

Javier shuddered. 'Four hours. That's how long he was on the toilet in his trailer one day. I gave up waiting to film a scene and went for a beer.'

He turned around and pulled out plates from a cupboard. He'd found his way around this kitchen better than she had. Just how much time had Javier spent here?

'A beer? You eat *and* drink? Well, you're just a Hollywood novelty.'

Javier put the eggs down in front of her, then searched through a few more cupboards. 'Yes, I eat. I know the damage it causes when you don't eat. Sorry, can't find the salt and pepper. Eggs and bread it is.'

He sat down opposite her with his own plate. Her stomach clenched. That sentence had just been thrown in there with the rest. Was he referring to his mother, or fellow film stars? Not eating was something that made the hackles rise on the back of her neck. A few years ago her sister Immi had suffered from an eating disorder. But that was the thing about not eating. It didn't just affect one person—it affected the whole family. Even now, every time she saw Immi the first thing she did was check her cheekbones, shoulder bones and her silhouette. Anything that might show any hint of trouble again.

She pushed the thoughts from her head, licked her lips and tried to keep the conversation going. 'I'm a terrible hostess, aren't I? I promise, once that water starts boiling, I'll make the coffee.'

He gave her a nod and she kept talking. 'So, how have you managed to stay away from the Hollywood madness, then?'

He raised his eyebrows. 'You haven't met my mother, have you?'

She shook her head. 'What was her name again? She modelled with Sofia.'

He nodded. 'Anna Lucia. She's around ten years younger than Sofia and I was a late baby. An unexpected surprise.' He picked up his fork. 'My mother is surprisingly traditional. She's seen all the madness of Hollywood and London. The drink, the drugs, the diets and general craziness.' He gave a little shrug. 'She won't admit what ones she trialled, but she's had her own problems.'

There was a change in his tone. It was only slight, but Portia picked up on it straight away. 'What kind of problems?'

He looked at her thoughtfully for a moment—as if he was trying to decide how to answer. 'We came here when my mother was stressed due to work.' He paused for a second. 'It didn't help at times that she was hounded by the press. Trapped in her home by reporters and photographers camped outside the house.' There was an edge of resentment in his voice and she shifted uncomfortably in her chair. He looked around himself. 'This place was good for her too. It calmed her. Brought her the peace that she needed.'

Portia's skin prickled. The words sounded so simple but the expression on his face was anything but. Guilt was swamping her. It felt as if he could see inside her heart and soul and knew that she was one of those people. The story chasers.

It made her uncomfortable. Especially when she wanted to reach out and touch his cheek right now. To offer some shred of comfort. 'And you came with her?' was all she could say.

He licked his lips. 'Most of the time. My father worked away a lot. When he realised my mother was getting unwell he tended to pack us both up and send us to Sofia.' He gave a half-hearted smile. 'I even went to school for a while on L'Isola dei Fiori. If you can call it that.'

'What do you mean?'

Javier shifted in his chair. 'Sofia arranged for me to be schooled "with friends" as she put it.'

'And who were the friends?'

'Alessandro and Nico del Castro.'

Portia started to choke on her eggs. Had he really just said that out loud? 'You went to school with the Princes?'

Javier looked nonchalant about it. 'Only for a few months until my mother was better. Sofia didn't want me to fall behind at school so she arranged for the palace tutor to include me in the lessons.'

'You were friends with the Princes?'

A black shadow crossed his eyes as she realised her mistake at once. Sometimes her press brain asked the questions before she'd had time to edit them. 'Nico, not so much. He was younger. But Alessandro, yes. There was only a year between us.'

Portia gulped. Alessandro had died two years ago. He and Nico had been cousins, but Alessandro was an only child, meaning Nico was now the heir to the throne.

'That must have been hard.'

Javier met her gaze with his grey eyes. 'Yes, it was. We weren't as close as we'd been as children. Alessandro was quiet. He didn't like the spotlight. The bright lights of Hollywood didn't suit him. But he visited a few times.'

Portia nodded as the water in the pot started to bubble. She got up to make the coffee. 'That's quite a difference in childhood. One part with glamorous Sofia and the Princes, and one part handyman with your Uncle Vinnie.' Javier Russo would be a biographer's dream. Why hadn't he done that yet?

He made a strangled kind of noise. 'Don't kid yourself. Small boys aren't glamorous—we spent most of our time conjuring up trouble. And Uncle

Vinnie? He was probably my blessing in disguise. He kept me on the straight and narrow. He taught me discipline.' He gave her a cheeky smile. 'Let's face it, there are a number of my co-stars who could probably benefit from some Uncle-Vinnie-style hard work.'

'Oh, I don't doubt it.' She spooned the coffee into the cups and poured the boiling water on top, taking care not to spill it.

'So what about you?' he asked as she pushed the cup towards him.

'What about me?'

She was surprised. Again he was catching her unawares. It was clear that part of the conversation had come to an end. Javier Russo was good at hinting without giving too much away. She was almost sure she could name each of the co-stars he'd been referring to when he talked. And the part about his mother? She'd just tucked it away somewhere. Probably alongside the older male film star who hadn't come out, and the depressed female film star. Already it felt too personal, too deep. The kind of stories she'd spent the last year pretending she hadn't heard.

'How many sisters do you have?'

She mopped up some of her egg with the bread. Sisters. The easiest topic in the world for her. She could talk about her sisters for hours. 'There are four of us. I'm the oldest, then there's the twins, Imogen and Miranda—she's the one that just got married—and then there's Posy—real name Rosalind—she's the ballerina.'

He paused for a second. 'The names—they're all Shakespeare characters. Were your mother and father fans?'

She nodded. 'They met at the Royal Shakespeare Theatre in Stratford watching *Romeo and Juliet*. My mother said it was fate. They took us there a few times as kids.' She shook her head and laughed. 'Posy tried to get up on the stage and dance at one point.'

'And she's the one that inherited the house?'

Portia nodded. 'Sofia was Posy's godmother. My godmother wasn't quite so exotic. She was my aunt, my dad's sister, and lived about two minutes away from us.' She gave him a smile. 'Sofia was always much more exciting.'

He nodded. 'Oh, I know she was. I saw some

of the parties.' He looked thoughtful. 'Your sister must be very disciplined if she's a ballerina. It's every bit as cut-throat as Hollywood.'

Portia pressed her lips together. 'To be honest, I think it could be worse. I'm not sure how happy Posy is. She's been in the corps de ballet for a while now.' Portia put her hand on her chest. 'Now, personally, I think Posy is the best dancer they have. But I might be a little biased.'

'Really?' Javier was sipping his coffee. He looked amused. 'What about the others?'

'Well, Miranda's a pilot. Cleve, her new husband, is a pilot too. Their wedding was just perfect. When they stood in the garden and said their vows it was gorgeous. I can honestly say I've never seen my sister so happy. It almost made me believe that true love might actually exist.' There was a little pang in her chest. She hated to feel envy. But the love and connection between Andie and Cleve had been crystal clear. 'And Imogen…' Portia paused for a second, trying to find the right words. 'She works at my dad's company, Marlowe Aviation. She's planning on getting married soon too.'

Javier looked at her curiously. 'Why did you say it that way?'

Portia sucked in a breath. 'What way?'

Javier put down his cup. 'You don't want her to get married.' He was looking at her curiously. Had she really been so obvious?

Portia thumped her own cup down on the countertop with a little more venom than she meant to. 'That's not true.'

'Really?' He smiled as he picked up the plates and carried them to the sink. He completely ignored her outburst.

He kept talking. 'What I'm not sure about is whether you think you should have got married first, or if you don't like the guy that Imogen is marrying.'

Portia was shocked. And Javier still had that look on his face—the one the world had fallen in love with, half joking, half serious. The expression that had drawn women in all over the world. But right now Portia wanted to dump her coffee over his head.

'That's a terrible thing to say. How dare you?'

She tossed her coffee cup in the sink, trying to ignore the loud crack. Oops.

'Well, which one is it?'

Darn this man. He wasn't going to let it go. The words stuck somewhere in her throat. The truth was she'd never liked Immi's intended. She never had. She never would. There was just something about him she couldn't put her finger on.

But she'd also already had horrible irrational thoughts about being left on the shelf and pictured herself with grey hair—a sad old spinster, sitting on a rocking chair like the one on the terrace, watching her sisters' families playing all around her.

Irrational. She knew it. But that didn't mean it wasn't there.

Anger surged through her. 'None of your business.'

Javier gave a little jerk backwards at her words. His amused, playful glance left his face.

She turned and strode out to the terrace. By the time the cool sea breeze started blowing her hair across her face she could feel a little wave of panic.

She was supposed to try and keep Javier sweet. She was supposed to be looking for some insider gossip that could help her keep her job.

But already things weren't sitting comfortably with her. What was it about sharing a house with a Hollywood heartthrob to make you feel like the only reject in town?

She was trying to be cool. She was trying to be professional.

She was trying to be underhand.

Ugh.

Her interview style had always been forthright, if occasionally flirtatious. Trouble was, just being around Javier was unsettling.

Maybe it was those grey eyes, sincere one moment as if the world were on his shoulders, and smouldering the next, as if any second now he would just push her up against a wall and kiss her as he had done his co-star in the last movie she'd watched.

She was pretty sure that had been rated the hottest scene on film that year.

And now she was living it—if only in her head.

Pathetic really.

She sensed him walk up beside her, shoulder to shoulder.

She was watching the azure-blue sea—perfect on a sunny day with waves rising in little white peaks of froth and crashing onto the rocks below.

'I'm sorry, I didn't mean to get personal.'

She licked her lips and begged her brain to find some nice, rational thoughts.

'I didn't mean to get shirty.'

He turned towards her, his brow furrowed. 'Shirty?'

The joys of language. 'Snappy. Impatient.' She waved her hand as his brow started to unfurl. 'Generally just a bit badly behaved.'

He smiled and nodded. 'Ah, well, maybe we're both a bit badly behaved.'

He was trying to be nice—she knew it—but, boy, did this guy speak in double entendres.

He stretched his hands out towards the perfect sea. 'How about I finish some of the more delicate plasterwork and we have a picnic on the beach in a few hours? I miss swimming in the sea around here. I haven't done it in years. It would be nice to bring back some memories.'

She glanced sideways at him. He looked contemplative. Thoughtful. Maybe he would be able to share a little with her once they knew each other better.

She nodded. 'I can get started on some cleaning. I'm going to wash some of the dust sheets and clean some of the windows in the rooms. How about I meet you back here in a couple of hours?'

He nodded and gave her a smile.

She licked her lips as she watched him walk away. In theory it all sounded fine. But the image of Javier Russo all wet in a pair of trunks had suddenly made her mouth go very dry.

Very, very dry.

CHAPTER THREE

HE WASN'T QUITE sure what it was about her. But Portia Marlowe was proving to be a little unexpected.

Javier had never been someone to believe his own press. Every film set, every job he worked on he got to know people from the runners, to the catering staff, to the executives who liked to visit for around ten minutes.

The film-star tag was a whole different ball game. He played the game when he needed to. He did the interviews. He'd even been conveniently photographed on occasion. The sexy label made him laugh out loud. He was comfortable around women. Usually, he had no problems communicating with them.

But he always kept a distance. He always controlled what was going on. He'd seen what the press had done to his mother. In a way he blamed them for her bipolar disorder. Most of her life she'd kept it under control. But when the press had decided to harass her, the stress had exacerbated all her symptoms. The sleeplessness. The fatigue. Her coping mechanisms. Her moods. Her erratic behaviour, coupled with her irritability and her inability to complete tasks—sometimes even sentences.

He'd been determined to always keep his press under control—to only let them know what he wanted them to know. The truth was he always mistrusted the press.

Portia? She was a little different. His mother had once described an English counterpart as 'prickly'. Today, it seemed to fit the bill. Prickly Portia. He wasn't quite sure how old she was, but he'd surely hit a nerve with her in the kitchen today. He wasn't usually so clumsy around women. His mother would have been horrified by him. Sofia would probably have slapped him around the back of the head.

He was getting little flashes of memories about her. There was something achingly familiar about Portia that he couldn't quite put his finger on.

Maybe it was the occasional way she said a word with her English accent that was pushing his buttons. He loved that accent. Not that he would tell her that.

He'd come here for some peace. He needed to figure out what came next in his life. From the second he'd got that phone call about Aldo he'd known that things would never be the same. He'd known that *he* would never be the same.

The biggest ache for him was the final diagnosis. Aldo was bipolar.

His friend had suffered from the same disease as his mother and Javier hadn't picked up on it. They hadn't spent a lot of time together in the last year. And Javier had been aware that Aldo had been low after the breakdown of his marriage. But that had seemed almost natural. Almost understandable. But Javier had missed the highs that Aldo had also displayed. The erratic behaviour. The despairing lows. Things that would have helped him put the pieces together to get Aldo the correct diagnosis and treatment before it was too late.

He'd already decided he wanted to do something specific for people with the same disorder. For families with loved ones who were suffering and didn't know how to help.

He just hadn't managed to decide the best way to do it.

This was his time out. His chance to gather his thoughts, arrange his finances and look at his calendar of work for the next year to take time to devote to this. Working on the house would have been therapeutic. He just hadn't expected the house to be filled by Portia Marlowe.

He sighed and walked through to the painted drawing room.

The plasterwork had to be done slowly. And once plaster was mixed it had to be used within a certain time frame. The long snaking crack across the dome had taken some gentle sanding and filling. He'd need to examine it again tomorrow. But now he picked up his wide range of trowels, hawk and scarifier to clean them before he used them again.

Upstairs he could hear the shower running. The dust must have got to places that he didn't even want to tease her about and by the time she came downstairs again he'd finished washing his tools.

Her hair was still damp, coiled around into a bun at the back of her head. She was obviously wearing a swimming costume but had a black sheer kaftan over the top and a pair of flip-flops on her feet.

He shook his head and pointed to them. 'Remember, we've got to get down that path to the beach. Do you have something else?'

She nodded. 'Oh, yeah, I hadn't even thought about that path. I have a pair of trainers I can wear.' She glanced over at him. 'Do you need to get ready?'

He glanced down at himself. A few blobs of plaster had landed on his grey T-shirt and three-quarter-length khaki shorts. He held up his hands. 'I got an award last year for best-dressed male.' He shook his head. 'I have no idea how that happened. They obviously don't know me at all.'

Portia crossed the kitchen and picked up the rest of the bread. She opened the fridge and came out smiling, holding a bottle of water with a little condensation around the outside. 'Look, it's decided to work today. We can take the rest of the bread, the ham and I have some cheese too.'

Javier had reached the door to leave but ducked his head back around. 'What, no wine?'

Something flitted across her face. 'I suppose we could if you wanted.' She ducked back into the fridge. 'Yep, there's some white. We'll take that.'

A few minutes later he'd washed his face and changed his T-shirt. He'd neglected to bring swimming shorts, but the beach was private and he was sure his black jockey shorts were respectable enough.

Portia had a couple of towels over her arm as well as a bag with the food. They made their way down the path to the beach. The stone was crumbling in places, and the path a little steep. A few times Portia's hand landed on his back as they headed down the slope.

The white sand practically sparkled. Javier kicked off his trainers and almost let out a yelp. 'Wow. It's hot.'

Portia smiled as she kicked hers off too. 'Well, it is brilliant sunshine—what do you expect?'

He looked at her skin. Her English rose complexion had seemed to gain an LA tan. It was light golden brown but she still looked as if she could burn easily. 'Are you all right being out in this sun?'

She winked at him. 'Factor fifty. Haven't you heard? I live in LA. Sun is a crime against skin.'

He laughed. 'You mean you haven't tried one of the crazy remedies?' He tapped his face. 'To stop wrinkles and regain youthfulness.' She burst out laughing as he mimicked one of the other popular male film stars who'd just filmed a TV ad for moisturiser.

There was a glint in her eyes as she laid the towels down on the sand. 'Which one? The elephant's urine? The fungus? Or the sixty-day-old-egg recipe?'

He shuddered. 'Is that the latest fad?' He waved his hands. 'My last co-star paid over a thousand dollars for some fish-egg cream. The smell—' he shook his head and screwed up his face '—was so horrendous, none of the crew would venture near her trailer.'

Portia started laughing as she walked towards the waves. 'And you had to kiss her?'

This time Javier exaggerated the shudder. 'I would never speak badly of a co-star. Thankfully, by the time we were filming, the cream was washed off and her make-up was firmly in place.'

Portia let out a little yelp as she paddled at the edge of the sea. 'Yikes, it looks so inviting but it's bitter cold.'

Javier grinned as he strode into sea. It was a little colder than he expected but it was exactly what he needed. He started sloshing the cold sea water over his chest and back. He turned around as he was doing it, letting the waves gently lap up to his back.

'Come on,' he gestured to her. 'Get in.'

She shook her head and pulled up the hem of her black sheer kaftan. 'Oh, no. Not yet. Paddling is as good as it gets.'

He squinted at her as she stood in the sun.

She laughed as the waves lapped up her thighs. 'How is it that as soon as you put a toe in the sea, it seems to try and drag you in further?'

His stomach clenched a little. Press. It was easy to forget that Portia was press.

But he couldn't forget it. He had to remember—at all times.

He had to be nice to her. If he wanted to stay here—he had to keep her onside. But he could still do that by keeping her at arm's length.

Today was only about being polite. The work might seem like a bonus for Portia, but for him it was therapeutic. He could think while he worked. He could make plans while he worked.

There was something about Portia. Maybe it was because she was press. But he could see it hidden behind her careful glances at him. She made his spider sense tingle, and that helped him remember she was the enemy. He got the impression there was more to Portia than met the eye.

He watched her as she took a few steps in, changed her mind and took a few steps back again. 'There should be a law against water this cold,' she muttered, her kaftan poised around her thighs. She took another few steps in, then shook her head. 'Nope. Not for me. Changed my mind.' She gestured towards the water. 'You swim. I'll watch. How about I promise to phone for help if I see you being eaten by a shark?'

She let her kaftan drop and waded out of the water to drop on one of the towels. She lay back and pulled her sunglasses down from her head.

'How are you going to do that with no phone signal?'

She waved her hand and sighed. 'Yeah. Not the best plan. Don't worry. I'll think of something.'

He shook his head and started swimming. He didn't notice the cold as he stroked out towards the buoy. It was only around half a mile out from shore and he'd swum this distance many times over the years. He kicked hard and got into the rhythm. No phone signal. And no Internet around here—although there might be a chance of Internet in town. Maybe he didn't need to worry about Portia too much. He reached the buoy and started back to the shoreline. It was easy to get into the rhythm. And this was a much better workout than heading to a gym. One of his favourite workouts back home was swimming at the various beaches around Los Angeles and he was spoiled for choice.

It didn't take long to reach the shore again and he waded out and dropped down next to her, rolling onto his back.

They were right in the middle of the white sandy beach. The naturally formed arch curving over them and offering just the slightest shade.

'It's safe,' he said. 'No sharks. At least not the sea-faring kind.'

She frowned at him but didn't question the statement.

'Lovers' arch,' he said. 'You know what they say about that.'

She rolled onto her side to face him and leaned her head on her hand. 'We didn't call it Lovers' arch. We called it Neptune's arch. That sounds much more exotic. Sofia called it that.'

He sighed and leaned a little closer. Close enough to cast a shadow on her face. 'I know. Don't tell anyone, but I actually preferred the Greek god Poseidon. His legend was much more interesting than the Roman god's.'

Portia looked over her shoulder and whispered, 'I think around these parts that might be considered treason.'

He put his hands behind his head as he looked up at the arch. 'Why? L'Isola dei Fiori is neither Italian nor Greek. For all we know they have their own ancient legends here.' He looked over at her. 'Do you remember the legend?'

She nodded as she reached for the bag of food. 'Sure I do. Neptune had found a lover, a woman on L'Isola dei Fiori. When we were children we used to joke it was Sofia.'

Javier nodded. 'I could imagine that.'

Portia pulled out the bottle of wine and opened it. 'But Neptune's consort, Salacia, was furious and called the other gods of the Underworld.' Portia poured the white wine into glasses. 'The woman—I can't remember what her name was—was heartbroken when Neptune said he had to leave her or she would be killed. He blasted the cliff with his trident, creating the rock arch, and told her that whoever kissed under the arch would find their true love.'

She handed one of the glasses to Javier and he propped himself up a little. He actually liked teasing her. It seemed that some clichés were true. The English were more uptight than Italian women and Portia was no exception.

'And have you ever tried to find your true love?'

She took a sip of the semi-chilled wine. She pointed back to the terrace on the cliff above. 'As children we often spied on the beach at night. If you were here during any of Sofia's parties you must have known that, at some point, all paths led to the beach.' She rolled her eyes. 'I'm just glad there are no lights down here. I think we would have seen a whole lot more than we should have.'

He nodded in agreement. 'I saw a proposal under here once.'

'You did?' Now that had captured her attention. She sat upright on the towel. 'Who was it?'

He shook his head. 'It was nobody famous. A pair of locals.' He glanced around. 'There must be a secret way onto this beach that no one knows about. Sofia and my mother were on the terrace drinking champagne cocktails when we spotted the couple under the arch at sunset. The guy kissed her then dropped onto one knee and proposed. Sofia was so excited she shouted down and invited them up to the villa for some champagne.'

'Wow. Do you have any idea what happened to them?'

He grinned. 'I might have. Let's just say I know twenty years later they're still together and living in Baia di Rose.'

Portia gave a sigh and took another sip of wine. 'It's a beautiful story.' She tilted her head to one side as she looked around. 'I've always been surprised that no one has tried to snap this place up.'

'What do you mean?'

'I just mean that this whole place—L'Isola dei Fiori—it's beautiful. It's breathtaking. And yet it doesn't seem overrun by tourists.' She gestured towards the arch. 'It's even got its own legend. In any other place there would be a multimillion-pound resort built on this coast with weddings held at the arch at sunset every night. What with the headline-stealing King Ludano years ago I'm surprised that L'Isola dei Fiori didn't turn into the next Monaco or Cannes.'

Javier couldn't help but laugh. 'You old cynic. But I can tell you one reason why it didn't.'

She looked curious. 'Why?'

Javier took a drink of his wine. 'Simple. No cinema. Can't do film premieres without one.'

Portia looked around her as if she expected a cinema to just appear out of the sand next to them. 'There isn't a cinema in Baia di Rose? Really?'

'Oh, there is now. But there wasn't then. Around fifteen years ago they converted one of the old theatres into a cinema—but all they really did was put a screen at the back of the stage. Up until that point the only place that had a cinema was the palace.'

'Really?' Portia sat up a little straighter. He tried not to smile. He should have guessed the reporter in her would suck up any snippet of information that could turn into a story.

'Yeah. Alessandro and I used to sneak in when the adults were watching movies. And not all of them were meant for children.' He tipped his head back. 'It was probably the thing that sparked my interest in film. Let me think, twenty years ago I can remember watching *The Rock*, *Jerry Maguire* and *Independence Day*.' He gave her a joking stare. 'And you have no idea how much I wanted to be a Borg in *Star Trek*.'

'Wow, was that really twenty years ago? It just seems like yesterday. We went to London to watch that at the cinema. Posy was mad. *The Nutcracker* was on at the National Theatre and she definitely didn't want to watch a sci-fi movie. I can remember the expression on her face as if it were yesterday.'

Her words struck a pang somewhere in his heart. She laughed as he topped up their wine glasses, and looked out at the perfect azure sea. In the distance there was one tiny white blip, a boat far out at sea. To all intents and purposes it almost felt as if they had the island to themselves. He picked up a handful of sand and let it run through his fingers.

Time. The one thing he'd discovered he didn't have enough of, until it was too late.

Aldo's suicide had been a bolt from the blue.

They'd been friends since childhood, grown up together, met girls together, got into trouble together. When Javier had started to have some success in acting, he'd flown Aldo out a few times to some of his locations. But over the years those times together had diminished.

Aldo had married. Then divorced. He'd lost weight and been quieter. On the times that he'd seen him, Javier had asked if he was well, if he needed anything. But his childhood friend was much too proud to talk—which had left him in tatters when he'd found out that the last person Aldo had called was him. What if he'd answered the phone? What if he'd managed to get a signal and called back later? Would it have made a difference? Would a conversation have been enough to make Aldo reconsider?

News of the suicide had left him reeling. Standing next to the graveside while Aldo's sister sobbed her heart out had torn him apart. He'd never forget the expressions on Aldo's parents' faces. Two broken people that could never be put back together again.

Javier's mother had insisted on coming too, but had turned up in an Italian grey silk suit, which had wilted and clung in the heavy rain. The weather had matched the mood of the people attending.

There were a few old school friends. But Javier hadn't been sure if they'd been there to pay their respects to their old friend, or to spy on the now famous one. It had left a bad taste in his mouth.

For weeks after the funeral Javier had been haunted at night. Going over every conversation, every email, wondering why he hadn't picked up on the hints that Aldo was unwell.

It had been seventeen months since they'd actually seen each other. Seventeen months. In a world of social media and live streaming that now seemed awful that he hadn't made more of an effort to stay in contact with his friend.

His simple excuse was he hadn't had time.

And his gut twisted at how truly pathetic that made him feel.

How many signs had he missed because he was moving on to the next film, attending an interview or press conference, or discussing deals with his agent? If he'd just stopped to ask Aldo the question—how are you doing? *Really asked.* Could he have made a difference for his friend? If he'd had a conversation with Aldo's family and heard about his behaviour would he have recognised the signs?

If he'd answered the phone that night and realised how down Aldo was—what would he have done?

The thought had played over and over in his head. He couldn't have left the film set. He'd been under contract and in the middle of the desert wasn't exactly easy to get away from. But he might have spoken to Aldo's sister—or tried to find him a doctor that could help him. A counsellor to talk to. Anything.

He'd never really spoken to anyone about this. Aldo's sister's tear-streaked face had been enough. 'You were the last call he made,' she'd said. 'What did he say to you? Did he give you any clue?'

His reply felt so worthless. 'I never got the call, Estelle. He just left me a message. I was away filming and by the time I came back…' He let his voice tail off. It was easier than letting her know how guilty he felt. Guilty that the message had said Aldo really needed someone to talk to. And his oldest friend had forgotten to call back.

He'd come here to reassess. Re-evaluate his life. Villa Rosa was his haven. His time out.

But from the moment that he'd got there, he'd got the distinct impression that it was Portia's haven too.

He studied her as she sipped her wine. Long dark curls with sun-tipped ends, light golden tan, long legs—mostly hidden—snub nose and—when she wanted to—a dazzling smile.

In lots of ways Portia Marlowe really was the perfect woman.

If only she had another job.

Not that he could even contemplate a relationship right now. In the last two years he'd only had time for a few dates, and none of them had made him want to plan ahead.

The press hadn't picked up on Aldo's suicide. He'd been relieved. The last thing Aldo's family needed was a reporter poking into their private business.

A few lines in a couple of online reports had mentioned Javier had flown to Italy for a funeral. But it had been the lead up to one of the biggest award ceremonies at the time and there had been a hundred other scandalous stories to fill all the papers and magazines.

Portia sighed and turned towards him. He leaned forward and topped up both of their glasses with wine, handing hers back to her, then turned to face her too.

For a moment time seemed to stand still. Both lying on their towels, facing each other with heads propped on their hands and white sand beneath their toes. The craggy rock arch had thrown a shadow over part of Portia. Her black kaftan had moved as she turned, revealing a long expanse of tanned leg. The rest of the thin material flickered in the breeze, hinting at all the curves underneath.

She looked at him with her big brown eyes and took a sip of her wine. 'I'm a musical girl. Which doesn't help in Hollywood these days when they don't make them any more.'

He smiled at the easy subject matter. Portia was wise enough not to pry, and to give him a little space.

'I always wanted to be one of the kids in *The Sound of Music*. I may even have longed for a pair of red shoes like Dorothy in *The Wizard of Oz*.' She moved her feet in the sand. 'If I click my heels three times I'll get back home.' She closed her eyes just for a second. 'You're not ready to go back home?'

'No. Of course not. This is a holiday.' Now he was curious. 'You said it was your sister's wedding last week—and you have a few weeks' holiday. How did you manage to get so much time off?'

It was a natural question. Everyone knew that in Hollywood unless you were constantly on the TV you were instantly forgotten. One of LA's late-night talk-show hosts refused to take holidays. His predecessor had taken holidays and by the time he'd come back from a round-the-world cruise he'd been replaced. Hollywood was definitely fickle and he was quite sure there would be another, equally beautiful and ambitious, woman snapping at Portia's heels.

'I was due holidays. My producer knew that. I've always filled in and covered emergencies for them.' She raised her eyebrows. 'I've even presented the weather a few times despite the fact I can't tell one cloud from another.'

He laughed. 'I can top that for jobs we're not qualified for.'

She gave an easy smile. 'How?'

'When I was a jobbing actor I was an extra on an old Western made-for-TV movie. I was supposed to just sit in the background of the bar, then walk past with horses a few times.'

'And?'

He gave her a wink. 'If you look in the credits you'll see my name under "Old Hag".'

Portia spluttered then choked on her wine. 'What?'

'Hey!' Javier flung up his hands. 'I got a line out of it. It was worth it.'

'What was the line?'

He wrinkled his face up and leaned close to her. Portia leaned in a little too, waiting for him to whisper. She was almost holding her breath, waiting to hear the line.

He couldn't resist. He took a deep breath, his lips close to her ear. 'It was…' he pulled back—

just for effect '...*"Stop thief!"*' His voice echoed across the beach and cove.

She fell back, tipping her wine over the sand as laughter shook through his whole body.

She slapped his shoulder. 'You ratbag.'

He winked. 'I might not have been the star, but it got my name on the credits. And the make-up was spectacular—even my own mother didn't recognise me.'

She tilted her head to the side. 'Where is your mother these days?'

He felt himself bristle. It was a natural question. It was him that had mentioned her. 'She lives in Rome these days.' He picked up his wine glass that was wedged in the soft sand. 'Here, have mine.'

Her fingers brushed against his as she reached for the wine. 'Thank you, I will. I think you owe me for that.'

'How can I make it up to you? Do you want me to sing to you? A duet? Break into a musical routine? I once made an attempt at the chimney-top dance from *Mary Poppins*.'

She rested back on her towel. 'Oh, I'd love to

see that. I'd pay money to see that.' But she shook her head. 'Although I love musicals, Posy's the one with all the dance talent. As for my singing? I can clear a room with a few notes.'

'That good?'

She nodded. 'Oh, yeah.'

This was the first time in a long time he'd actually felt relaxed. Actually wanted to be in a woman's company. Maybe it was Villa Rosa? Maybe it was the fact he knew he could do manual labour for a few days and clear his head. Or maybe it was the sometimes prickly woman with the best accent and the biggest brown eyes he'd ever seen.

She gave a sigh as she looked out across the ocean. 'The view here is just amazing. I always thought my favourite place in the universe was the Griffith Park Observatory.'

'You like it up there?' He was surprised. It was a popular place in LA. He just hadn't thought of it as a place Portia would visit.

'The view across LA is amazing. And the view at night?' She held up her fingers, blew a puff of air into them and flicked them in the air. 'It's just mesmerising.'

He gazed across the azure sea. 'As good as this?'

'Hmm...' She contemplated for a second. 'I guess they could be equal.' She lay back and looked up at the arch. Her eyes took on a wicked twinkle. 'You do know that Sofia wanted to paint the arch pink—don't you?'

'What?' He sat bolt upright, then shook his head and started laughing. 'No way. No, she didn't.'

Portia gave a firm nod. 'Oh, yes, she did. It was one of her phases. She thought the arch would look better in pink. My grandmother nearly had a fit.'

He turned around to face her again. 'I guess it never came to anything.'

She took a drink of her wine. 'Thank goodness.' She squinted up at the arch. 'Can you imagine if this had been painted *pink*?' She gave a shudder.

He couldn't help but smile at her. Portia was nowhere near as prickly as he'd first thought. She might even be fun.

'How about I make dinner tonight?'

Her eyes shot up for a second. Then she gave him a knowing smile. 'Are we barbecuing?'

'Why?'

She grinned. 'Because I'm not sure how reliable the oven is. You can cook on the stove—I've made a few mean omelettes in the last week—but that's it.'

He shook his head. 'You've survived the last week on omelettes? Oh, no. Surely we can do better than that. There are a few restaurants in Baia di Rose—why don't we see if I can arrange a taxi and head to one of those?'

She bit her lip. It was almost as if she were contemplating saying no. When was the last time a woman had turned him down? He almost couldn't remember.

Getting out for dinner might do them some good. He needed to head into the village anyway to order some glass for the conservatory. Having dinner seemed like a plan.

It might also help him keep his guard up. Being in a house with one person made things very informal. It tempted him to forget that Portia was a reporter. Particularly when she was lying next to him on the sand looking like this.

Her hair was tied back with some kind of clasp, with a few loose strands blowing in the breeze around her face. If he leaned forward right now, he could brush that hair back with his fingertips and just touch his lips against hers…

He couldn't help it. He reached over and trailed the tip of his index finger down her nose. Her dark eyes widened and she licked her pink lips.

Something clenched around his heart like a fist. A conversation. Rearing up from the back of his memory out of nowhere. Aldo. Telling him about the first time he'd kissed Lissa. Telling him he'd known straight away that she was the girl he was going to marry. He'd never seen his friend so happy. He'd teased him for months about the devotion to his wife before they were married. Before it had all fallen apart.

Could he really have made a difference?

He pulled his finger back, trying to forget the softness of her skin beneath his touch. He didn't deserve this. He had no right to reach out to

Portia—and find even a second of happiness—when Aldo couldn't do that same.

A whole host of memories flooded through him again. *Sleeping with the enemy.* It was only a figure of speech but that was what this equated to. What on earth was he thinking? Portia was press—and press should always be kept at a safe distance.

His movement was sudden and Portia bit her lip, confusion flooding her eyes. She pulled herself back out of his reach, gathering up the glasses and bag from the sand.

'It's getting too hot for me,' she said quickly, her voice wavering slightly. 'I think it's time for me to go back inside.'

He cringed. What was he thinking? One second he wanted to be in her company, the next he was thinking about what he'd lost. He was so conflicted right now.

Guilt overwhelmed him. It might not be rational. It might not be justified. But it was just where his head was.

No matter how much he wanted to he couldn't turn back the clock.

He couldn't go back and have that conversation with Aldo.

And until he made peace with himself and put the steps in motion to make a change—he certainly couldn't do anything else.

CHAPTER FOUR

PORTIA WALKED OUT of the room and he sucked in a breath.

She was wearing a belted pink dress that shimmered and black stiletto heels. Her hair was pulled back from her face and tied in a bun at the back of her head and she was wearing bright red lipstick.

He hadn't moved. It was as if a warm breeze had just enveloped his skin making every tiny hair stand on end. There was something achingly familiar about the way she looked.

'I've seen those clothes before. That dress—it's striking. Is it a US designer?' Maybe one of his co-stars had worn the same dress at a photo shoot.

She took a long time to answer. Her hand ran across the satin material of the dress. 'Maybe at the awards ceremony. This is the dress I wore for the red carpet interviews when we met. It's not designer. I found it in a vintage dress shop a few years ago. I threw it into my case when I came for my sister's wedding in case I needed something more formal to wear.'

Her posture had stiffened and she wasn't quite meeting his gaze.

The awards ceremony. He'd tried to smile and be sociable but inside he'd felt as if he were dying. One of his co-stars had muttered beneath her smile that he was being inexplicably rude.

His mouth felt dry. The night had passed in a blur to him. He couldn't remember a single part of it. He'd still been in shock. Still trying to get his head around what had happened.

Doubtless Portia had been one of the people he'd been rude to.

He licked his dry lips as his stomach coiled in a way it hadn't in a long time. He felt like a kid in a headmaster's office. 'Did we talk on the red carpet?'

The look she shot him told him just about everything he needed to know. She waved her hand dismissively and walked past him. 'I don't think you could call it that.'

He caught her by the shoulder, stopping her in her tracks. 'Portia, wait. I'm sorry.'

She spun around, fire dancing behind her eyes. 'Really?' The word was spoken like a challenge.

'I wasn't myself that night.'

She tilted her head. 'Oh? You weren't? The arrogant man I met that night wasn't you?'

He cringed. He should have known. Portia was prickly. It was clear he had offended her. 'I'm sorry.'

'You're sorry? For asking me if that was the best I could do?'

She was angry with him. That much was crystal clear. He shook his head. He couldn't even remember what he'd said. But he did recall feeling exasperated by the never-ending questions that night about the film, his co-star and his suit. It had all seemed so superficial—so unimportant.

She was facing him now and he put his hand back up on her shoulder. He spoke softly. 'Please. I was upset. I couldn't concentrate on being at the ceremony.'

She frowned. 'What do you mean? That's the biggest night in any actor's career—whether you're nominated or not.'

She was right. He knew she was right. Connections made on awards ceremony night could lead to great things—if your head was in the game.

He could feel all the barriers he'd put up earlier start to crumble. He knew she was a reporter. He knew he should be cautious. 'I'd just lost a friend. I'd just come back from the funeral.' He didn't add any more. He didn't want to reveal any more about the situation.

'I didn't know that.' She seemed surprised.

He gave a wry smile. 'Not everything reaches the gossip columns.'

She met his gaze and leaned towards him a little. 'And not every story that I hear makes the news.'

She was right under his chin now. The light in the corridor was dim and her pupils had dilated, making her eyes even darker than normal. Her voice was breathy. As she stepped closer her jasmine scent wound its way around him. He could hear one of the old-fashioned clocks ticking in the distance, marking the passing of time.

It was a simple sentence. But he could see a whole host of other things on her face. Conflict. Learning. She was a reporter. This kind of thing was her job. But how many secrets did Portia know that she hadn't shared? He'd never even contemplated that before.

'Isn't it your job just to find the next story?'

They stood in the dim hall for a few seconds. He was conscious of her breathing, of the rise and fall of her chest under the pink shimmering material. His finger itched to reach out and touch her skin.

But he resisted. He couldn't do that. He didn't want to start something he couldn't continue.

It felt as if they stood there for a while. Neither moving. Both of them wondering what could come next.

She met his gaze. 'That depends on me. I'm not as hungry for a story as I used to be. I won't let myself be pushed in directions I don't want to go. Hollywood lost its gloss for me a long time ago. We have a saying in Britain that today's headlines are tomorrow's fish and chip paper. It's Hollywood. There will always be countless affairs and scandals. I don't worry about revealing cheaters. I don't worry about breaking news about who has got the next big role in a blockbuster movie. But even I have morals. There are some things I won't tell. Ever.'

He was kind of taken aback at the declaration. She'd obviously listened when he'd revealed his dislike of reporters earlier. He hadn't invited Portia for dinner tonight in the hope that something would happen between them. Just the opposite.

He'd hoped that in a formal environment it would be easier to remember who she was. Too bad they hadn't even reached the restaurant yet. Because she seemed to have turned all that on its head.

He couldn't help the attraction that was simmering beneath the surface. Right now he wasn't even sure he wanted to.

Portia licked her lips and took a step to the side. 'I think that was our taxi.' She smiled.

'It was? I didn't even hear it.'

He stepped back and put a smile on his face, making a sweeping motion with his hand. 'Ms Marlowe, can I take you to dinner?'

He strode over to the main door and reached for the handle just as she did too.

Their hands brushed together again. Somewhere, in that last romantic movie he'd made, the film director had just cut to include multicoloured fireworks in the distance. He could practically hear them exploding next to his ear.

Portia pulled her hand back. 'Sorry.' He could almost see something change in her eyes. There was a glimmer of determination. Where had that come from?

He watched as she sucked in a breath and tilted her head towards him.

'About the awards. You were cheated. You should have been nominated yourself.' Even the pitch of her voice was different. It was as if she'd just moved back into Hollywood reporter mode.

It changed the atmosphere in the air between them.

But he couldn't help but smile. 'I appreciate

the sentiment. But no, I shouldn't. That film was terrible.'

He could tell she couldn't help it—her shoulders started to move and then her suppressed laughter bubbled over, her hand at her mouth. 'You think your own film was terrible?'

He laughed as he opened the front door for them just as the taxi pulled up outside. 'Sure, I do. At least, I was terrible. My co-star had a much better part than I did.'

'Then why on earth did you make it if you didn't like it?'

He wrinkled his nose. 'My agent told me to. He said the film was clever. He thought it was more *art nouveau* than anything else I'd made. He said it would widen my audience appeal.'

She rolled her eyes. 'Like that's what you need. Just about everyone in the world knows who you are.'

He opened the door on the taxi for her. 'And that's not always a good thing. Anonymity can be nice.'

She gave him a curious stare as she climbed in the taxi. 'If you say so.'

* * *

The journey in the taxi took less than five minutes. Javier was wearing dark trousers and a white short-sleeved shirt. The evening was warm so neither of them had a jacket, which meant that in the confines of the vehicle the dark hairs on his arms were practically tickling her skin. She was flustered and she hated being flustered.

It wasn't a normal state for Portia Marlowe. She spent most of her time in front of the camera, cool and unruffled.

She was about to go out to dinner with Javier Russo. The film star currently adorning a thousand teenagers' walls.

What on earth was she going to say?

Javier chatted easily in Italian with the taxi driver, asking him questions then taking a piece of paper and scribbling some notes before handing it back. She blinked as he pulled out his wallet and took out a wad of cash. 'What's that for?' She looked around—not quite sure what she was looking for—but almost as if it was some kind of clandestine act.

Javier laughed. 'The taxi driver lives next door

to the builder's merchant. I've asked him to get me some glass for the conservatory. He's going to bring the delivery to Villa Rosa tomorrow.'

'Oh, I see.' She gave a sigh and flopped back against the cool leather of the two-seater. Her brain was spinning. What was wrong with her?

From the second he'd touched her cheek on the beach her brain had been filled with a thousand thoughts. She'd been straight with him. She'd been in Hollywood too long. She'd been propositioned by some actors, and seen others cheat and betray. She was jaded. And while the attention Javier was giving her was flattering, she also had the tiniest belief in the back of her mind that she could be being played. After all, wasn't Javier one of the best actors around?

The taxi driver opened her door and she stepped out. Javier had chosen a small restaurant overlooking the port. The waiter showed them to a table on the terrace without so much as a blink. Portia reached up to grab a strand of hair and twiddle it around her finger. It was a nervous habit—one she'd had since she was a child. But she'd forgotten her hair was coiled tightly into a bun at the nape of her neck.

Did no one else recognise Javier? She glanced around the restaurant. It was exactly as it should be. There was a large family at one table, and two other couples at tables on either side of them. Both couples were completely engaged in conversations with each other. No one seemed to have noticed their resident film star.

Javier pulled out a chair for her. 'Would you prefer inside? Will you be too cold out here?'

She shook her head quickly. Inside the restaurant was lit by flickering candles. Much too intimate. Javier gave her a nod. 'Would you like some wine?'

She nodded quickly. 'Rosé?' he asked as one eyebrow arched jokingly.

'No, white, please.' The waiter had placed a menu in front of her but her eyes had caught sight of a wooden board listing their special for the evening. 'I think I'll have the fish. White would suit better.'

Javier looked over his shoulder and nodded at the board too. 'Ah, yes, the fish looks good. We'll both have that.' He handed the menus back to the waiter and pointed to something on the wine menu. 'And this, please.'

The waiter nodded and disappeared. Portia felt her stomach do a little flip-flop.

She was out for dinner with Javier Russo. And those sexy grey eyes that usually graced the big screen were looking straight at her. Javier looked completely relaxed. He glanced around the port, watching the bobbing boats and fishermen packing up for the night. His head nodding slowly.

'Do you recognise this place?'

'Of course, I spent hours here as a kid.'

She was surprised. 'You did?'

He leaned forward and put his elbows on the table. 'You didn't?'

Portia shook her head. 'Hardly ever. We mainly just played at the house or on the beach.'

Javier gave a little smile. 'You and your sisters were obviously good girls. I couldn't wait to get a bit of freedom and wander into the town.' He pressed his lips together for a second, 'The house was either too quiet, or complete chaos.'

She was tempted to press for more. 'Didn't you enjoy spending time with Sofia?'

He looked out over the water. 'Well, yes, and no. The days could be long for a small boy.'

'You weren't playing with the Princes?'

He raised his eyebrows and she burst out laughing. 'That didn't quite come out right.'

He shook his head. 'No, I didn't play with the Princes. I didn't meet them at first. It was only when we had to stay for a bit longer that Sofia made the arrangements with the tutor. Even then, I always knew I was persona non grata in the palace. Alessandro was quite reserved to begin with—not like Nico at all.' He smiled and shook his head. 'Even now, every time I hear Nico's name, I wonder what crazy sport he's up to now.' He picked up the fork on the table and passed it from hand to hand. 'Alessandro would have been a good King.' He looked out over the port again. The sun was beginning to lower in the sky sending streaks of orange and red across the water. 'He loved L'Isola dei Fiori. He wanted the absolute best for this place and its people.'

He looked up and met her gaze for a second.

'Parents just shouldn't outlive their kids. There's just something so wrong about it.'

There was an ache to his words. A pain. Was he talking about Alessandro's death and the fact his father Vincenzo was still on the throne, or had Javier lost a child himself?

Almost instantly a cool breeze swept over her skin and she shivered. The waiter chose that moment to appear and pour their wine. She'd never been so glad to let the dry, sharp taste fill her senses.

Javier paused for a few seconds, sipping at his wine and staring at the horizon.

Her stomach did another flip-flop. If Javier had something deep and dark in his past she wasn't sure she wanted to know. She liked the Javier Russo that the world did. His sexy smile, the glint in his pale grey eyes and the way he could look at you as if you were the only person on the planet.

The flash of pain there had unsettled her.

She was looking for a headline. Something that could cause a five-minute frenzy, and let her get in her boss's good books again. But as tempting as that could be, she'd meant it when she'd told him that not every story made it onto her entertainment show.

Just being in Javier's company meant the questions she'd already been asking herself about her job seemed to be magnifying in her brain. He wasn't acting like the arrogant man she'd met on the red carpet in March. She'd brushed off his explanation—but maybe it had been true?

Javier turned his attention back to her. She could almost see him switch off—push the thoughts he was having away.

He leaned on the table again. 'So, Portia, what are your plans for the rest of this week?'

She smiled as the waiter set down their plates and she picked up her fork. That was a couple of times he'd done that with her. It seemed Javier had learned the art of changing the subject well. 'I haven't decided. I'm split between just cleaning in general or going up into the attic and starting to find out what's up there.'

'Knowing Sofia, it could be anything.'

She sighed. 'Part of me is excited, and part of me is dreading it.'

'Dreading what?'

Portia poked at the fish in front of her. It looked wonderful, it smelt fantastic, but her stomach was still doing flip-flops. She pressed her lips together and gave Javier a smile. She closed her eyes, seeing the villa in all its splendour in her head. Sofia in a beautiful long green satin dress, gliding down the staircase with a glass in her hand. Guests mingling all around her, spilling out through the conservatory and onto the terrace. Others gathering in the flickering candlelight of the domed room. 'Dreading getting rid of all the memories of Sofia,' she admitted. She opened her eyes again. Javier was looking at her with the strangest expression.

She shrugged. 'When I first walked into the villa I just...just...*felt* her. You know? It doesn't matter that she's been gone two years. When Miranda walked up the stairs of the villa and opened the door of the wardrobe, revealing her spectacular clothes, it was like being five again. I kept expecting Sofia to walk in behind us and offer us a piece of her jewellery to match her clothes.'

'You were wearing Sofia's clothes?' He looked puzzled.

Portia nodded. 'Sorry, yes. Miranda got married on the beach below the house. It was kind of short notice. There was no time for bride or bridesmaid dresses. We all just picked something out of Sofia's vintage wardrobe.' She finally took a bite of the fish—it was delicious.

'You did?' He seemed genuinely surprised. 'I thought the wedding dress was a big thing for you girls.'

'Oh, it is.' She nodded. 'If you want it to be.'

She picked up her wine glass and took a sip. A smile crept across her lips.

'What? What is it?' Javier's eyes were sparkling.

She shook her head. 'I'm just thinking about some of the celebrity weddings I've covered.' She leaned across the table conspiratorially. 'Honestly, you have no idea. If an average woman can turn into a bridezilla, what do you think a Hollywood star with a million dollars can do?'

He wrinkled his nose. 'Bridezilla?'

She waved her hand. 'You know—a crazy lady. Thinks the whole world revolves around her, and her wedding.'

He nodded and smiled. 'Okay, I've got it.'

'Let's face it. It doesn't matter how much money you spend on a wedding—or where it is. It's the person you marry that's important.'

He gave her a thoughtful glance. In the dimming evening light those grey eyes were mesmerising. People always said that every photo of a star these days was edited. And for the majority of them that was true.

But for some reason, right now, Portia had never seen a more handsome man in her life. The exposed skin on her arms prickled at the mere thought. The white shirt showed off his tan perfectly. She could see the hint of stubble on his jaw. Her fingers wanted to reach across the table and brush against it. The edges of his lips started to hint at a smile. 'So, what you're telling me is that you're a romantic at heart.'

She gave a conciliatory nod. 'I guess I am. I've never seen Miranda look happier. Cleve too. I guess a year ago he thought he'd never be happy again.'

'Why, what happened to him?'

'He lost his wife in an accident.' She ran her

fingers up and down the stem of the wine glass. 'Grief can be a horrible thing.'

Javier was watching her closely. 'Do you think that people can have more than one big love in their life?'

She was surprised. Not many guys she knew would ask a question like that, and she wasn't quite sure how to answer. She nodded. 'If you'd asked me before, I would have said no. I would have said that I thought there's probably only one true love out there for everyone. But now? When I watched Miranda and Cleve say their vows together I could see the love in their eyes—their devotion to each other. I think they're lucky that they've found it.'

Javier gave a slow nod. 'So, Portia—no big love in your life?'

She shifted a little in her seat. This conversation was getting very personal. Wasn't the shoe supposed to be on the other foot—wasn't she supposed to be getting information from him instead?

She sighed. 'In LA? Not a chance. Most of the time life feels unreal there. You must get that.

I'm so busy with work most days that I don't really have time for dating. I cover all the parties but I don't actually *go* to them.'

She didn't want to seem too cynical, but the truth was her experience of Hollywood was a sham. After all she'd witnessed in the last few years she'd completely shied away from dating anyone around Hollywood. It all seemed so false. Why risk your feelings or your heart when it would end up broken anyway?

Javier laughed. 'Oh, come on. You're telling me that *none* of my fellow actors have ever invited you into one of the parties?'

She raised her eyebrows at him. 'Of course they have. And I don't need to tell you who they were—you could probably list them. But I'm not *that* kind of girl.' She took another sip of her wine. 'What about you? You get photographed often enough. Who is your latest flame?'

Are all your relationships fake too? That was the question she really wanted to ask.

He shook his head. 'No one—much to my agent's disgust. If I'm not photographed every few weeks with a different girl he seems to think my star will fade.' It was clear from the way he said the words that he wasn't at all bothered. That surprised her. She'd always thought there was a hint of arrogance around Javier. But here, in Baia di Rose, he didn't seem like quite the same person. Her curiosity was piqued again. He'd mentioned being at a funeral. Maybe the loss had affected him?

She filed the thought away and stuck to the conversation. 'So, how many of those photographs have actually been real?'

He winked. 'Let's see how good you are. How many do you think were real?'

She leaned back in her chair and tried to remember who he'd been seen with. After a few moments' contemplation she met his gaze. There was a twinkle in his eye. She counted off on her fingers. 'Okay, your co-star in the action film, Olivia Burns—no way. The comedy actress, Linda St John—' she waved her hand from side to side '—maybe. The female wrestler Jill Cacanna? No way, and last but not least, the up and coming Ms Ruby Delaware? Yes, I think that one might have been real.'

Javier started laughing. 'Oh, dear. Olivia, yes. But that was never going to last. Linda? No. We're just friends. Jill? Best blind date I ever had. She's one of the coolest human beings on the planet—but it's impossible to have a relationship when you never see each other. And Ruby?' He looked thoughtful for a moment and tapped his fingers on the table. 'That was odd. I think I might have been played.'

Portia was astonished. She thought her instincts were usually pretty good. But not with Javier Russo it seemed. What was it about him that just seemed to boggle her senses?

'What do you mean "played"?'

It was clear he was a little uncomfortable, and that reassured her a little that he wouldn't normally be indiscreet.

He reached for the wine bottle in the cooler at the side of their table and topped up both of their glasses. 'I'm not really a "drop a note to the press" kind of guy.'

She understood instantly what he meant. Lots of celeb photos on the beach, or coming out of restaurants, were staged—everyone in their industry knew that.

'But I think my agent is.'

She racked her brain trying to remember who Javier's agent was but came up blank.

'You think your agent was involved?'

He sighed. 'I'm not entirely sure. I think there may have been chat between my agent and Ruby's. All our time together felt kind of stage-managed. I didn't notice at first. But after a while, you realise that every time you go somewhere—even if it seems spontaneous to you—there are paparazzi waiting. It just didn't sit comfortably with me.'

Portia was amused. Ruby was a pretty enough actress. 'You think she wasn't actually interested in you?' It just seemed ridiculous. Javier was one of the hottest guys around. She just couldn't imagine that. But even more surprising was the fact that all his relationships hadn't been fakes. It seemed she didn't know everything about Hollywood after all.

'The truth is I don't know. She was nice enough but I always got the impression that underneath that sweet smile there was a streak of ruthless ambition. Once we started dating and had been photographed a few times she landed a couple of roles in upcoming blockbusters. It wasn't that she wasn't already being considered.' He stopped for a second, obviously trying to find the right words.

Portia finished the sentence for him. 'It's just that the exposure probably helped boost her up the list a little?'

Javier visibly cringed. 'I think so. It made me stop and take stock. Well, that and other things.'

He was doing it again. Fixing his gaze on the horizon while his thoughts obviously went elsewhere.

She didn't think she was boring him.

Please don't let me be boring him.

Javier Russo was more contemplative than she would have guessed. She'd only scratched the surface but was sure there was a whole lot more going on underneath.

She wanted to press. She really wanted to press. But her stomach gave an uncomfortable twist—

almost as if it were acting as her conscience. It just felt…wrong.

'What about your agent?'

That caught his attention. He looked back at her again. 'What do you mean?'

She lifted her hands. 'On one hand, they're working well for you. You've had good roles.' She smiled. 'Or almost good roles, in back-to-back films. Isn't an actor's greatest fear not working?'

He nodded.

Just like mine, she thought.

'But, if your agent is involved in playing games with you—manipulating you—is that really what you want?'

Javier blew out a long slow breath between his lips.

She saw it as opportunity to continue. 'You said they wouldn't be happy about you having a break. Maybe not. You're probably the person they make the most money from. But, on the other hand, if you're their most bankable star, shouldn't they be looking after you *more* instead of less?'

He let out a gentle laugh and leaned across the table, his hand covering hers. The warmth shot up her arm like an electric shock. Someone at the next table was pointing at them, obviously recognising who Javier was. 'Portia Marlowe,' he whispered, 'you ask all the right questions.' He gave her arm a tug and pulled her up, throwing some money down on the table with the other. He was still smiling. She saw someone lift their phone at her side. Javier's hand was still holding hers, the other had casually snaked around her back, pulling her hip against him. His face was only a few inches above hers and he was grinning at her. 'But I like it. You're making me think. And that's exactly what I'm here to do.'

He glanced at the road between the restaurant and the port. 'Come on, it's a beautiful night. Let's walk a little.'

He didn't wait for her reply, just kept her hand in his as he led her out of the restaurant.

It was as if something had changed in the air between them. That physical contact was doing weird things to her brain. He'd taken her hand so easily, so casually, but should he really be holding it? All she knew was there was no way she was tugging it back.

As they walked along the port she noticed a few curious glances in their direction. Her heart skipped a few beats. Javier pointed out a few familiar places from his childhood. He seemed more at ease here, more relaxed. He nodded at the few people who said hello. Portia was trying her absolute best to be as casual as possible even though she felt as if there were a huge red arrow above her pointing to their entwined hands.

The breeze was warm, joined by the laughter of those drifting out from the nearby bars and cafés. The horrible tense knots that had been in her shoulders since she'd got here slowly started to unknot. L'Isola dei Fiori had a peaceful feeling around it. She hadn't really noticed it as a child.

When she was a child it had been a place of wonder and amusement.

Now she was an adult it was different. It was the first time in a long time that Portia had walked down a street where everyone didn't have a phone pressed to their ear. People were actually looking at each other, and talking to each other. In LA that was practically unheard of.

Javier was easy to talk to. He asked more questions about her family and her father's aviation business. He wanted to know where she'd gone to university and where her favourite holiday resort was. But as soon as he started to ask about work, she felt herself prickle.

'You were the one that broke the Jake and Meg affair, weren't you?'

She nodded. That particular story had been one of the biggest scandals in Hollywood a few years ago. Two of the biggest 'happily married' stars who'd had an affair together on set on their latest movie. Both of them were regularly talking in the media about how much they loved their partners, constantly talking about family values. The reality of their lives had been a little different and most of the world didn't believe it when the story first broke.

It was yet another nail in the coffin for love in Hollywood. It seemed that it just didn't exist out there.

'How did you find out, anyway?' His hand was still holding hers and as they walked he'd shifted his thumb so it was tracing little circles in the palm of her hand.

She gave a shrug. 'Would you believe a mistaken text message? It seems that Meg Malone and I had mobile phone numbers with two digits interchanged.'

His eyes widened. 'Do I want to know what the message said?'

She smiled and gave a shudder. 'Oh, no, absolutely not. The only reason I figured out who it was, was because they mentioned being interviewed together on a talk show that night. I did a little digging after that and…' She held up her hands.

He gave his head a shake. 'Well, I didn't know anything about it. I was just as surprised as everyone else.'

Portia let out a long slow breath as they kept walking. They'd reached the outskirts of the town and the villa wasn't too far away. 'I got offered the job at Entertainment Buzz TV permanently after that.' Her chest constricted. The thought of going back to LA in a few weeks with no story made her feel sick.

Her job would be no more.

What would she do next? Where could she find work?

That tiny little voice was rattling around her head. *Push Javier. Dig deep. See what you can find out.*

But the thumb making circles in the palm of her hand was stopping all rational thoughts.

She'd spent the last five years not being fazed by film stars, then, she'd arrived in L'Isola dei Fiori, spent one minute in Javier's company and felt like a star-struck teenager all over again. And that feeling wasn't really going away.

But part of her brain wasn't thinking about Javier the film star any more. It didn't matter that he could be the ticket to keeping her job.

Javier, the teenager that worked with his Uncle Vinnie, the young boy with the sometimes sick mother, was revealing a little more about himself every time they spoke.

He only let go of her hand when they finally reached the villa and slid the key in the lock. She couldn't help it, her feet led her automatically back outside, through the conservatory and out onto the terrace. The pinks and blues of the sky had vanished, leaving a navy dark sky dotted with little twinkling stars. The breeze here amazed her. Any time before she'd been on the coast the sea winds had always been fierce, no matter how mild the weather. But the breeze here was warm and welcoming, moving through the surrounding gardens with a mere rustle. The white sand in the cove gleamed beneath her, shadowed only by Neptune's arch. It really was the perfect place.

With the perfect person.

She heard his footsteps and felt his presence just behind her.

'Why are you so tense?' the voice whispered in her ear.

She stopped looking out over the horizon and closed her eyes for a second. She'd been tense since the first second she'd arrived here, first of all worried her sisters would figure out something was wrong, then, secondly, worrying about sharing a house with a Hollywood superstar.

She couldn't help the fact that the tension and anxieties in her head automatically translated their way into her body. She hated feeling like this, she really did.

She gave a little gasp as two firm hands found their way onto her shoulders. The fingers started moving straight away, finding the tiny knots around her neck and shoulder blades. She wanted to tell him to stop, but she could feel his warm breath at her neck and sense the presence of his body inches behind hers.

She moved her head from side to side as he continued. 'My goodness. What have you been doing? You're coiled tighter than a spring.' His soft Italian voice was like a soothing balm.

As he kept working his fingers she could visualise the picture from this morning, the bare chest and shoulders, the chiselled abs and dark hair. Then again from tonight, the twinkle in his grey eyes, his tanned skin and white smile. She moved without even thinking, leaning her body against his.

This time it was Javier that gave an intake of breath. His hands moved from her shoulders, one resting at the side of her waist. He rested his head just above one shoulder, taking his other hand

and tracing one finger from the nape of her neck, painstakingly slowly across the top of her shoulder and down the length of her whole arm.

It was like a million little butterflies beating their wings against her skin. For a second she couldn't breathe. Then his fingers intertwined with hers and wrapped in front of her, resting next to her stomach.

His voice was low. 'I think that Villa Rosa has a little magic in it. Healing powers. It's a place to relax. To enjoy.'

She nodded, enjoying feeling his skin against hers. She couldn't pretend that her tension was gone. It had just been replaced with a whole other kind of tension.

She hadn't dated in so long. When was the last time she'd actually kissed someone? Sometimes, even though there seemed to be sparks flying, one kiss could reveal everything you needed to know. And right now her lips were tingling in anticipation. It didn't matter that Javier was behind her. It didn't matter that this probably wasn't the best idea she'd ever had.

He didn't seem to like false relationships any

more than she did. He didn't want to be played—and she was still surprised he'd experienced it. It made him seem less movie star, and so much more human than the arrogant man she'd had in her head from months ago.

She leaned back a little more, letting her breathing match the rise and fall of his chest. Were the healing powers Javier was talking about for her, or for him?

She still hadn't figured out why he was really here. Then again, she hadn't told him why she was really here either.

It seemed they both had something to hide.

But right now, with Javier's arms around her and their breathing in sync, staring out at the dark sky, the world seemed perfect.

'I could stay like this forever,' she whispered.

'Me too.' His reply sounded wistful and it sent little pangs throughout her heart.

So she settled her head back against his chest and they just stood, watching the dark sea stretching out in front of them, the glistening of the sand beneath them and the twinkling stars up above.

* * *

He'd almost kissed her. Two nights ago he'd almost turned her around and kissed her.

But as the warmth of her body against his had started to flood through his system he'd been struck by the fact that Aldo couldn't kiss a beautiful woman any more.

Aldo didn't get to do anything any more. And until he'd figured how to deal with that, he couldn't possibly get involved with anyone.

Which meant he had to apply his energy elsewhere.

The last two days Portia had continued to clean the upstairs rooms, emerging every now and then with smudges on her nose and cheeks. The glass had been delivered at the villa and he'd spent the last two days measuring, cutting and replacing individual panes of glass.

It was painstaking work but—as the plaster needed a few days to fully dry—it worked out well.

The conservatory was gradually beginning to take shape and regain some of its lost splendour. So far he'd only replaced the clear glass. The coloured glass he'd leave until last—because that was the glass that took the conservatory from elegant and sophisticated to dazzling and unique.

As he tidied his equipment he sighed. He needed to make a few calls. One of the deals he'd just reneged on was with a director he had a good relationship with. Javier knew he'd landed back in LA last night and would prefer to take the time to talk to him in person to explain why he'd backed out. He'd also like to talk to Aldo's parents—and the only way to do both of these things was to go into the village and find a phone.

Things were starting to take shape in his head. He had a few ideas. What he really needed to do was talk them over with someone he could trust. But there was only Portia here right now. And if he wanted to talk his ideas through, he'd need to give her the background.

Telling a reporter about Aldo's suicide seemed like the worst idea in the world.

'Portia?' He strode to the bottom of the stairs and shouted up to her. She appeared within seconds, wearing pink capri pants and a white shirt knotted at her waist. She had a list in her hand.

She waved it at him. 'I'd just been taking a note of a few cleaning products I need to pick up.' She wrinkled her nose. 'We need some food too. I was planning on heading into the village.'

He gave a guarded smile as a few more thoughts processed in his head. 'Great minds think alike. I have a few errands to run. Let's take the scooter.'

She narrowed her gaze for a second. 'Okay, but who gets to drive?'

'You want to drive?'

She held out her hands. 'It's sunny, I'm in Italy and there's a scooter sitting in the garage. Of course I want to drive.'

He shrugged. 'Then I guess I'm in your hands. Let's go.'

It had been a strange few days. The time on the terrace had felt magical—at least to her. But just when she'd thought something might happen, Javier had backed away as if he'd been stung.

She'd gone over and over the moments in her head. Nothing had happened. Nothing. Of that she was sure.

But it had still stung. It still felt like rejection.

She'd spent the last two days being polite and mannerly with Javier. Maybe she'd misread the whole situation? Maybe Javier had never even considered kissing her and it was all just a figment of her imagination.

That made her feel uncomfortable. She hadn't imagined the way he'd looked at her. She *hadn't*. Or the sparks in the air between them.

But for the last two days she'd cleaned. And cleaned.

Villa Rosa was finally starting to emerge from the clouds of dust.

She finished off her list and closed down her computer in the kitchen. Javier walked in at her back. 'Are you writing something?' He looked a bit uneasy.

She waved her hand. 'It's nothing. Just a story I've been working on for a couple of years. It helps me focus.'

He looked at her inquisitively. 'What kind of story takes two years to research?'

Something clicked in her brain. 'Oh, it's not a report. It's not *that* kind of story. It's fiction. I'm writing a book.'

His eyebrows rose. 'You're writing a story? What kind of story?'

The computer was closed now. She smiled and folded her arms. 'I'll let you guess. What kind of fiction writer do you think I am?'

He paced in front of her for a few seconds. 'Let's see. Thriller? No.' He shook his head and kept pacing. 'Historical? Hmm…no. Not that either. Romance?' He wiggled his palm. 'Maybe. Women's fiction?' He gave her a quizzical glance. 'Now, if I had my way, it would be science fiction or fantasy.' He turned to face her. 'But no, I think it's a romance. Am I right?'

She couldn't help but give a little smile. It felt ironic. 'You think I'm a romantic?'

His answer was automatic. 'Shouldn't we all be?'

She shook her head. 'It's not exactly romance. It's more Hollywood bonkbuster. I used to read them as a teenager and absolutely loved them. They've kind of gone out of fashion lately. But you know what they say.' She shrugged her shoulders. 'Write what you know.'

She picked up the keys to the scooter. 'Ready to go?'

He nodded and fell into step next to her as they left the house and headed to the garage. 'You are going to let me read this at some point, aren't you?'

She laughed as she slid her leg over the seat. 'Well, that depends how hard you work. Now, get on. The sooner we get to the village, the sooner we can get back. I've got an attic to tackle this afternoon.' She winked at him. 'Did I tell you that I crashed this once?'

'You what?' She was grinning, revelling in the fact he was horrified. 'What do you mean you crashed it?' He looked over the vehicle again. There were no obvious signs of damage.

She shrugged. 'You know, teenage girl, sneaking out in the dark to meet a teenage boy in the village…' She laughed. 'I ended up in a ditch. But I was more angry about the fact I'd ruined my favourite dress and taken the toe out of one of my shoes.' There was a mischievous twinkle in her eyes and he wasn't quite sure whether to believe her or not.

He shook his head. 'And there are four of you? How on earth did your father cope?'

'If you think I'm bad you should meet my sisters. I'll have you know that I'm probably the best behaved.' She winked again. 'Come on, slowcoach, get on.'

With her dark eyes and tumbling locks—and if her sisters were anything like her—he was sure that the Marlowes must have been the most popular girls in town when they visited.

He climbed on behind her, then paused for a second, before moving closer and putting his hands on her waist. 'Why do I feel as if I'm going to regret this?' he murmured in her ear.

She laughed, gunned the small engine and took off.

By the time they reached the village Javier wasn't sure he wanted to get back off the bike. He was afraid he wouldn't be able to stand straight.

Portia drove as if she were being chased by a pack of man-eating zombies. It didn't matter that the top speed of the scooter wasn't exactly law-breaking, she zipped around corners and snaked between cars fearlessly. She laughed as she jumped off and took off her helmet. Her cheeks were tinted pink and her brown eyes were gleaming. Her shiny brown hair fell back over her shoulders. He almost sucked in a breath.

Portia was always a pretty girl. But sometimes she just glowed. Like now. He tried not to focus on her lips. Her pink, distinctly kissable lips.

It was easy to forget other things around Portia. Most of the time she was good company and light-hearted. He couldn't believe that she didn't have a boyfriend back home—especially with the kind of job she had.

And she could actually eat. In LA that was practically a miracle. Lots of people in TV or film had their own personal trainer and chef and spent the day eating unappetising seeds, drinking green smoothies and timing their next workout.

Portia seemed happy in her own skin. He was intrigued about her writing. Next time they were back at the villa he was going to try and persuade her to let him read her bonkbuster. He had a feeling he might recognise a few of the characters.

She pulled sunglasses from her cross-body bag and put them on. 'Will we meet back here in an hour?'

'Sure.' He glanced around the village. He was pretty sure he knew where he could find a phone. He watched as she strolled off towards the fish-mongers, trying not to focus on the swing of her hips or the shape of her bottom in those capri pants.

He felt a huge pang of regret. He could have kissed her the other night. He *should* have kissed her the other night. But right now it just felt as if his timing was completely off.

He found a phone in the local café and made the calls he needed to. The director was disappointed but not upset. He understood that Javier needed some time. Aldo's parents spoke briefly. They still sounded vacant and it broke his heart.

It made him more determined. More focused on what he should be doing. The work on the house was therapeutic, but what he actually should be doing was putting words into action. Bipolar disorder. How many people around the world were actually affected? How many families? Would the average person recognise the signs? After all, he'd missed them—or at least he felt he had. There were helplines all across the world. But was there something specific for bipolar disorder? Or was that something that he could do in Aldo's memory?

It was time to stop being distracted. It didn't matter how dark those brown eyes were. It didn't matter how kissable Portia's lips looked.

The ache and guilt in his heart were still there. It was time to put all his focus on one thing.

The trouble with trying to stay incognito was that curiosity drove her crazy. She'd been in the village less than half an hour, the groceries in a bag at her side, before she found herself in an Internet café.

She wouldn't look at her emails. She wouldn't. She'd maybe just have a five-minute browse of the Web and see what was happening in the world. There was a geriatric TV in Villa Rosa, but the signal was pretty rubbish and, with no phone line or Internet, there was none of the digital services that went along with most modern-day TVs.

So, unless something made it into the relatively conservative Italian newspapers stocked on L'Isola dei Fiori, or into the Italian TV news, she was essentially cut off.

It was a mistake as soon as she sat down. She knew that. She just couldn't help herself.

She pulled up Entertainment Buzz TV's website and Holly Payne's white teeth, blonde hair and size-six figure screamed back at her. She was covering while Portia was gone and it looked as if she was planning on making her mark.

Portia signalled to the waiter for a drink. She couldn't do this without coffee.

She flicked back over the last week. Holly covering the latest film premiere. Holly interviewing an unknown actor who'd just signed to star in the film of the biggest selling novel last year. Holly covering the death of an old-time movie star.

Portia breathed an audible sigh of relief. There was nothing spectacular there. Nothing that would draw attention to Holly as anything other than another Hollywood reporter.

Just to be sure she put Holly's name into the search engine on the Web.

It literally exploded.

So much for no attention.

Is Holly Payne about to become Holly Parker? screamed one headline. There were dozens more like it—all from last night. It seemed Entertainment Buzz TV's website needed updating.

Heading the article was a smudgy photo—obviously taken on someone's phone. It wasn't great. But there was no mistaking the people. Holly had her lips on Corey Parker, the latest pop sensation. He, in turn, was leaning her backwards and kissing her in the middle of an LA club. Portia recognised it immediately.

She let out a laugh. Really? Holly pretended to be twenty-two. But Portia knew exactly how old she was—and that was seven years older than Corey Parker. She was just blessed with a youthful demeanour.

Portia peered at the screen again. Was that even a dress Holly was wearing? It looked more like a handkerchief. But the picture seemed to have caught one of Holly's best features—her legs—in all their glory.

Speculation was rife. There were hints at how long she'd been secretly dating Corey Parker. Rumours that she'd already met the family. Even more rumours that she and Corey had been seen checking out wedding venues. Really?

She blinked as she noticed something in the corner of her screen. What?

She sucked in a breath and sat back. Holly Payne's social media followers had just skyrocketed to three hundred thousand. Oh, no. *Oh, no.*

Her fingers moved without her brain really engaging, pulling up her email provider and automatically typing in her email address and password.

She hadn't been in her emails since she'd arrived on the island for her sister's wedding. She didn't even glance at the total number. She just pulled up the name she was looking for. There were seventeen from her boss at Entertainment Buzz TV.

She pulled her hands back from the keyboard for a second and picked up the coffee the waiter had delivered, trying to ignore the shake.

This was pathetic. She hadn't even opened any of them and she wanted to cry.

Her boss had been succinct as she'd left. *'Don't come back without a killer story.'*

It had played on her mind ever since. And with each passing day the nerves and racing heart seemed to multiply like a killer virus. It was the hint as well. The implication. Almost as if she wanted something sordid. Portia hated that. Her boss was pushing her in a direction that she didn't want to go.

Ping. She opened the latest email from her boss. What was the point of reading the rest?

Due to recent events our executive director has suggested it might be time to review the arrangements for lead presenter on Entertainment Buzz TV. As per your contract, we are required to give you four weeks' notice. That is unless, of course, you can bring us a story that generates as much publicity as our current Holly Payne/

Corey Parker headline. In those circumstances we would, of course, reconsider.

The breath left her body like a deflated balloon. She was a has-been.

Was it even worth going home at all? Her stomach twisted. She loved her LA apartment. She loved her friends. Up until a few months ago she'd loved her job. She couldn't quite work out in her head what had happened. Maybe she'd always known her sell-by date would be coming up soon. Maybe she'd always known that there were some stories that shouldn't be told.

But how could she pay for her apartment if she wasn't working? Her salary at the TV station had been good—where else could she get paid like that?

Her skin started to prickle. Maybe she should reconsider the scoops she already knew. The Hollywood actress famous for her smile. She'd always been intensely private about her life. Her young daughter was terminally ill. That was why she was depressed. That was why she'd had to seek help at a private clinic. But was that really something Portia could share with the world?

No. She just couldn't. If she did something like that she wouldn't be able to look at her reflection in the mirror.

What about the nearly ninety-year-old Hollywood classic actor—married three times but thoroughly gay? She liked him. She really liked him. He was like one of the last true gents. It all seemed thoroughly unfair.

Then, something else came into her head.

Something so ridiculous she wasn't quite sure how it got there.

Holly had landed Corey. What if she could land Javier Russo?

Javier was a much bigger star. The highest earner in Hollywood this year. He'd topped every Most Eligible list for the last few years. Being seen on the arm of Javier Russo was much more newsworthy. Being seen in a clinch with Javier Russo could send the Internet into meltdown.

She winced. It was ridiculous. Of course it was ridiculous. He was the most gorgeous man on earth. He wouldn't be interested in her. He could have kissed her at any point the other night—and he hadn't. The humiliating part was he probably hadn't even contemplated it.

And she couldn't help but wish he had.

Her cheeks flamed with heat.

She hadn't filled Javier in on the rest of the 'crashed scooter' story. The fact that she'd never even got around to meeting that guy in the village. She'd thought she was going to get her first kiss. Instead she'd ended up in a ditch. It was fitting really. Her sisters had all managed to squeal about first kisses long before she'd finally been disappointed by hers. As she was the oldest they'd all just naturally believed she'd gone first. She would have hated them to find out she was last.

She closed the window on the computer in front of her—not even bothering to send a reply email. There was no point. She had nothing to tell. In another week or so she could kiss her job goodbye. She stood up, left some money and walked out of the café.

A realisation was creeping over her. When she'd been given the ultimatum before she left she could have held her ground and refused to leave. She didn't believe that Holly had 'accidentally' met the latest pin-up. Every part of the situation was contrived. The whole thing was just so Hollywood. Holly had seen an opportunity and taken it—just as Portia had five years earlier. It was just that Portia hadn't done it in quite so spectacular a fashion.

She should be in LA. That was where all the stories were. That was where she could find a story that would let her keep her job. So why hadn't she stayed?

Her stomach gave a little churn. How could she have missed Miranda's wedding? It didn't even bear thinking about.

The truth was she'd been having second thoughts about her job—she just hadn't wanted to admit them even to herself. And now she was having third thoughts. Or even final thoughts.

She'd fallen out of love with her job. She didn't have the hunger for it any more. She wouldn't do *anything* to get a story.

Her stomach was tied up in knots. This was it. This was when she needed to make a decision once and for all about her job. If it was over, she needed new career plans—rapidly.

Getting to know Javier had confused her. Discovering he wasn't the arrogant film star who had a string of false relationships had been news to her. And even though she'd had that tiny fleeting thought about using Javier for a story, the last few days had given her clarity.

She wasn't that person. She couldn't be that person.

Javier had reasons for being here she didn't know about.

But it didn't matter what they were—if he ever revealed them she already knew she wouldn't share them with anyone. It was his business. Not hers.

She couldn't be underhand. She couldn't be deceptive around Javier. Maybe he'd been right to distrust the press in the past. But she didn't ever want him to feel that way about her.

She was so caught up in her own thoughts that she didn't even notice Javier striding down the street towards her. He had a strange look in his eye. He looked just as tense and as distracted as she was. The charm that she'd glimpsed earlier had vanished. He held out his hand for a second, and it took a moment for her to realise what he wanted.

She pulled the key from her pocket. 'I take it you want to drive?'

He nodded.

He swung his leg over and started the engine. 'Ready?'

She swallowed the huge lump in her throat. What she really needed right now was someone to talk to. But Javier wasn't that person.

Something had upset him. Just as something had upset her.

And it seemed that neither of them were ready to share.

CHAPTER FIVE

THE NEXT TWO days were awkward.

It was clear Portia was unhappy about something. She was distracted and tired-looking. Sometimes she even looked as if she could burst into tears.

He'd love to use her as a sounding board. When it came to work and Hollywood she was completely sensible and, at times, frank. He respected her opinion.

But he couldn't tell her why he was reacting in an emotional way. He couldn't tell her how guilty he still felt about the death of his friend, and why he was so mixed up.

Because Portia was press. And he couldn't wipe his past experiences from his head—the press couldn't be trusted.

Part of it was pure and utter selfishness. What if she thought badly of him if he told her? There was a definite attraction simmering between them. Nothing like telling her he'd ignored a friend in need to squash it completely.

It didn't help that the reason he was shutting her out was because he still felt a pull towards her. Something he didn't feel as if he had any right to act on.

In the meantime a plan had formulated in his mind. He now knew what he wanted to do. Money was no problem. But he wanted to make sure that he did things well—not just throw a bunch of money at the project and walk away. He wanted to be involved and that would take business plans and commitment.

He looked around the painted drawing room. He'd plastered the crack again, skimmed most of the other rooms in the house. The conservatory glass would all be replaced in a matter of days. But he had to be careful and take his time. The frame was delicate. He couldn't manipulate and replace too many small panes at once. So far he'd completed all the plain glass and added some random red, blue and yellow panes. The green, pink and purple glass panes were sitting in a corner, waiting for their turn to be anchored in place and transform the conservatory into a rainbow of sunlight.

Up above him he could hear some noise. Portia had disappeared into the attic this morning. Maybe it was time to try and smooth the path between them.

He walked through to the kitchen and made some coffee, finding some pastries he'd picked up at the baker's this morning. He knew better than to go empty-handed.

Portia Marlowe didn't take her pastries lightly.

She could smell the coffee before she saw him. In fact, a steaming cup of coffee and a delicious-looking pastry laced with chocolate were sitting on top of one of the trunks near the entrance to the attic.

She crawled forward on her hands and knees, reaching the entrance to the attic and sticking her head out of the door. Javier was sitting on the floor outside, sipping coffee from a huge mug. He was wearing jeans and a white T-shirt that seemed to be smudged with bits of off-white putty. She scanned the floor around him. 'What—no pastry?' She wagged her finger at him. 'Don't think I'll give you half of mine. Ask my sisters. I've never been very good at sharing.'

He shook his head as he sipped at his coffee again. 'I ate mine before I even came upstairs. You forget, I've seen you in the bakery before.'

She sat back on her haunches and sipped her coffee. It was strong—just the way she liked it. 'This is different. Did you get something new?'

He smiled. 'I bought some beans in the village this morning and a cafetière. What I really want is one of those giant silver coffee machines and my own barista.'

'Is my instant coffee not up to your standards?'

He pulled a face. 'I don't think it's up to yours, either.'

She nodded as she took a bite of the pastry. It was delicious. The chocolate melted on her tongue.

'I'll make do. I'm just glad for the sustenance.'

He nodded towards the attic. 'You look like you're having fun in there.' There was a glint of humour in his eyes.

'I do?' She looked down. Her pale trousers were covered in grime, as was her pink T-shirt. She put her hand up to her head and brought it back down covered in a large cobweb.

She was on her feet in an instant, jumping around and shaking her hand furiously. 'Yeugh. Get it off.'

Javier started laughing, a deep throaty laugh that seemed to come from deep inside. When she eventually shook off her hitchhiking cobweb and ducked into the bathroom and washed her hands, one glimpse in the mirror made her wince.

Why, oh, why didn't she have the natural look like the female movie stars? Her hair was all over the place and she had a large black smudge on her nose. No wonder he was laughing.

She wiped her face and went back to the hall. 'There's not much point in trying to clean up. I've got a million other boxes to go through in there. Trouble is, I'm not sure what I should be dumping and what I should be keeping.'

'Would you like some help?'

'Don't you have the conservatory to finish?'

He gave a casual shrug of the shoulders. He

had that expression on his face again, the half-smile that made a million women the world over go weak at the knees.

'It's a delicate operation. The frame is weak. I need to let the glass settle. I'll do the rest of the panes tomorrow.'

She gave a nod and folded her arms. 'So, are you going to be the brains of this operation—or the brawn?' She sighed. 'I have to be honest, I'm not quite sure what to do with some of the things—or most of the things—that I've found. I don't know if they're valuable or just junk. I think I've spent the last hour just moving things around.'

Javier took another drink of his coffee then set the cup down. 'Then let's get to work. I asked around. The waste-disposal trucks come tomorrow. If there's anything that we think could be disposed of, we can bag it.'

He pushed himself off the floor. She tried not to stare at his muscled biceps clearly defined by his white T-shirt. He walked towards her, stopping only a few inches away. She frowned and reached out and picked at the dried smudges on his T-shirt. 'What are these?'

He looked down. 'You're not the only one that needs a clean-up.' He pulled the T-shirt out from his chest. 'Some of it's silicone…some of it putty. Working with Uncle Vinnie taught me some bad habits. I tend to wipe my fingers on my shirt instead of on a rag.' He let his T-shirt flop back against his chest and her hand fell back on his warm chest. The heat was instant. She hadn't really meant to get so up close and personal. Her eyes connected with his.

It was like being hit by a blast. The smouldering heat in his grey eyes could never be mistaken for anything else. It took her by surprise as the blood instantly raced around her system. This hadn't been in her head. It wasn't her imagination.

She pulled her hand back as if she'd been stung. She wasn't quite sure how to deal with all this.

Javier didn't move. It seemed like the longest time but it must have only been a few seconds before he finally spoke. 'Let's get started. We can always go freshen up at the beach later.'

He brushed against her as he moved inside the attic. Her brain was spinning. The beach. The place where they'd drunk wine and he'd touched her cheek. The place she'd first felt a real connection with Javier Russo. Her lips tingled in nervous anticipation as she gulped and followed him into the attic.

There were two tiny windows in the roof of the attic that let a little murky light filter through. Javier had to crouch down in the roof space to try and get inside. He glanced over his shoulder at Portia and gave her a smile. The place was stacked with boxes, trunks, plastic bags and cases, there was hardly any floor space visible and he had to pick his way over and around them to get even a little inside. 'Did you know Sofia was a hoarder?'

Portia shook her head. 'Honestly? I didn't have a clue. And from what I can see, nothing has a label. I've only checked a few bags at the front and one case at the door. It's full of china all wrapped in tissue paper.'

Javier held out his hands. 'Where do you want to start in here?'

Portia shook her head. 'Your guess is as good as mine. Why don't you take one side and I'll take the other? It's probably best if we keep to near the front—that way, if we find anything that can be dumped, we can take it downstairs.'

He nodded and moved over to the nearest trunk. 'Okay, then, let's get started.'

Portia got back down on her hands and knees. There was no point standing—this was going to take a long time. The first few bags were easy. They were mainly filled with ancient household appliances. Kettles, toasters, scales, all singed or with bits missing. Portia pushed them towards the attic door, along with the next bag that was full of similar items.

Next was a large leather trunk. She flipped open the lid and tried to ignore the cloud of dust that puffed into the air around her. 'Oh, wow,' she gasped.

'What is it?' asked Javier.

The trunk was full of clothes, all in individual clear garment bags. She lifted out the first. A long red evening gown. The next dress was black, the next green and so on and so on. Portia smiled. 'I knew that Sofia had a lot of clothes but I guess I didn't realise quite how many. I thought the wardrobes downstairs held all her dresses. I hadn't figured on her having more up here.' She pulled the neck of the garment bag down a little to feel the red dress. 'Oh, it's gorgeous. These are probably worth a fortune.'

Javier was smiling at her.

'What? What is it?'

'You,' he said. 'You look like you just won the star prize.'

She sighed and held the dress against her chest. 'That's what it feels like. If we push this trunk outside I can take the dresses downstairs and find somewhere to hang them.' The smell of lavender was drifting up around her. 'They all look in perfect condition. Posy will need to decide what to do with them.'

'Posy—that's the ballerina, isn't it? Will she be interested in a whole load of extra dresses?'

Portia smiled. 'Oh, yes. Posy and I have similar tastes. She'll love these.' She met his gaze. 'It's strange. Posy and I are very close. When I was young and the twins came along, it was almost like they had their own secret language. They didn't really need me. They were so close. They didn't seem to want anyone else around. When Posy came along it was such a relief. Finally, a partner in crime.' She sighed. 'I love my sisters. I do. But even in adulthood Posy and I are much more similar. Immi and Miranda both went into the family business and Posy and I, in some way, both went into show business—albeit very different aspects.'

He was watching her and smiling. 'Do you talk often?'

Portia licked her lips before she answered. 'Andie and I spoke a few times when she was contemplating the whole Cleve thing.' She smiled. 'Posy—I'm a bit worried about her. She seems a little distant right now. And Immi?' She pressed her lips together. 'We've not really talked in the last few days. I think something's going on but I don't know what.' She shook her head. 'I always worry about her—always. I can't help it.'

'Why?'

She bit her lip. Immi's condition hadn't exactly been a secret, she just wasn't sure how much to share. 'Immi was unwell. She had an eating disorder when she was younger.' She paused then added, 'Then she had some mental health issues and ended up in rehab. It didn't just affect her. It affected the whole family. In a way I'm glad she's in the family business. It means there is always someone to keep an eye on her.'

She felt exposed. She'd just told him about her sister. It was private. It was personal. She'd got so used to the Hollywood lifestyle of everything just being on the surface that she'd forgotten how tough it was to share.

It left her feeling vulnerable. Something she hated.

His hand brushed against hers. It seemed accidental, but then it stopped and his warm hand covered hers, giving it a gentle but reassuring squeeze.

He hadn't said anything out loud to acknowledge her words, but the squeeze sent a little shockwave through her system. The more time she spent around this man, the more he crept under her defences.

Javier stared at her for a few seconds. Then he

lifted up a black and white photo in the trunk. It was a picture of his mother and Sofia laughing. They had their arms around each other and looked as if they'd just been caught sharing a private joke.

He looked into the trunk. 'Hey, what's this?' He pulled out something that was down the side of the trunk.

It looked like papers, but as he fanned them out she realised they were black and white photographs—all of Sofia. She picked up one after the other. 'Oh, look at her, isn't she so beautiful?' She kept flicking through in wonder. 'I never really remembered her like this. It's sad but you end up remembering someone the way they were the last time you've seen them.' Something about the pictures was familiar and it took her a moment to realise what it was. 'It's these! It's these dresses. Look, there's the black one. And this one is the red one—look how figure-hugging it is on her. And there's the green satin one all covered in sequins—look at the way it catches the light in the photograph.'

The pictures were fantastic. A little moment

in time. Sofia was spectacular in them, so elegant and refined-looking. And while she'd always looked immaculate in real life, she also had a wicked sense of humour and raucous laugh that took those that didn't know her by surprise.

Javier's hand closed over hers again. Reaching for the photographs and looking at them slowly, one after the other. He gave a sad smile. 'You're right. You do remember people the last time you saw them. And Sofia faded a little, didn't she?'

Portia looked at his sincere expression. Sofia had faded. She hadn't taken well to growing old. She'd hated the fact she had wrinkles on her face, or that her hair had thinned. She would never let anyone take photographs of her in the last few years. Javier had found a way to say it nicely. It was obvious he had the same affection for her that Portia and her sisters did.

Javier ran his fingers over one of the photos. 'These capture Sofia in all her crowning glory.' Then he burst out laughing. 'No, I think that might have been an unfortunate choice of words.' He shook his head. 'She never got her crown, did she? I wonder if she ever actually thought that she would.'

Portia bit her lip. 'I don't know. She would never have discussed anything like that with us. But she might have with your mother.' She looked into the distance. 'I always thought of her as fiercely independent. I never really knew that Ludano had gifted her the house. I didn't find that out until I was much older.'

Javier gave her another grin. 'Do you want to see what I've found?'

She tried to glance over his shoulder. 'Why? Is it something good?'

'I think you might recognise it.'

She put the photographs back on top of the trunk, trying to remember she'd need to email Posy about them, then crawled on her hands and knees over to where Javier had another large case opened.

He pulled out one of the items at the top. It was an old Italian Monopoly game. Portia gave a little shriek. 'Really? That's what you found?'

She couldn't help herself; she immediately started scrambling through the case, finding a whole host of other childhood games she used to play with her sisters. She pressed the well-worn box to her chest. 'We couldn't understand parts of it. We loved the names of the Italian streets, but when it came to the Chance and Community Chest questions we just had to guess what they meant. I'm sure that Immi used to cheat. Every time she got one, she said it was her birthday and we all owed her money.'

She looked in the case. It was packed full of things she remembered. She pointed at a few. 'We had a huge fight over that chess set. Miranda and I both wanted to be black—the knight especially in the shape of a horse was really fierce and we ended up stomping off to other parts of the house rather than play each other.'

Javier was looking at her thoughtfully. 'You have lots of good memories here, don't you?'

She nodded. 'We had the best times here.' She tilted her head to the side. There was something about the way that he'd said that. 'You must have had too?'

He opened his mouth and then hesitated. 'Well, yes, and no.'

She set the board game back down. 'What do you mean?'

She watched as he sucked in a deep breath. 'My mother wasn't always at her best when she was here. And I'm not sure Sofia knew how to relate to a young boy. She was kind. I was never neglected but—'

'But, what?'

He gave a tiny head-shake. 'I'm quite sure she had no idea how to entertain an eight-year-old boy. Then a nine-year-old, then a ten-year-old…'

He let his voice trail off then took a deep breath and spoke softly. 'My mother has bipolar disorder. At times in her life she's been quite unwell. In those days most people called it—what was it—"highly strung". But it was much more serious than that—particularly if she went off her meds. Sofia was good for her when she was like that. She would encourage her to take her meds and start eating again. Sometimes it took days, sometimes it took weeks.'

Her breath caught in her throat. It was the first time he'd ever really shared something so personal with her.

It was almost as if a wave of acknowledgement swept over her. 'How often was your mother unwell?'

It was the first time she'd seen him look kind of sheepish. 'She was at the height of her fame then. She was under a lot of pressure.'

He was making excuses for his mother. Even all these years on, as an adult he was still doing his best to protect her. She liked that about him, but it also made her ache for what he'd been put through.

She reached over and put her hand on his arm. 'And you were a young boy.'

He nodded. 'I was. But for some reason, even though my mother wasn't well, I still liked being here. This place. It's warm. And my mother always got better, and as she did she had more time for me. We walked on the beach. We took trips on the boats at the port.'

'What did she think of you being friends with the Princes?'

He laughed. 'Believe it or not, my mother wasn't too happy. She didn't like Ludano. She didn't think he was good for Sofia.'

Portia smiled. 'He probably wasn't. But it was different times then. There wasn't the same news reporting or social media that there is today. Sometimes I wish we could go back in time.'

'So do I.' His voice was wistful. He shook his head. 'Things were better here. On the mainland in Italy, my mother was hounded by the press. I can hardly remember a time when I could look out into the gardens and there wasn't a photographer hiding in bushes somewhere. Times were changing—even then.' He held up his hands. 'But here? Here was a little piece of paradise. A little bit of sanctuary for us all.'

She gave him a warm smile. 'It seems that Villa Rosa has lots of memories for us.' She looked around the cramped attic and held up her hands. 'This place. It's full of Sofia. Everything I see, everything I touch reminds me of her. How is Posy supposed to decide what she should get rid of? The other morning I woke up, and for a second, just for the tiniest second, I forgot that Sofia was gone. Then, in the blink of an eye I remembered again. It was like getting that phone call all over again. I know it sounds strange. I know it's ridiculous. But I wanted to sit in that split second—just for a while.'

She knew he didn't realise it—but it wasn't just Sofia she was talking about. It was everything. It was back to a few years ago when everything in her life had just seemed too good to be true. It had taken her until now to realise it had been.

Reality sucked.

Or did it?

The glamour had been fun. Some of the personalities had been fun too. She'd met a few of her all-time heroes. Some had disappointed. Some had lived up to and beyond her expectations. But times were changing for her too. She didn't feel the same fire, the same excitement about her job. She certainly didn't like the direction her boss had been pushing her in lately. She was spending longer and longer playing around with her writing. The words came easily—they just flowed. In a way she was glad that Javier was here. He was a welcome distraction. If she'd been here alone, her resolve might have crashed and she could have been back on a flight to LA by now.

She looked over at Javier. Something was

wrong. He looked almost grey. As if he were unwell. He was staring blankly at the wall as if he were lost in his thoughts.

She sat up on her knees and cupped his cheek with her hand. 'Javier? Are you okay?'

He blinked. There was a sheen in his eyes. Was Javier going to cry? What on earth had she said?

He put his hand up over hers, sending little shots down her arm. His head gave the briefest of nods. 'Yeah, I'm okay. Or, I will be.' He paused for a second. 'Portia, how do you feel if we take a break? Cool off down at the beach for a while?'

Her stomach curled up. He was sad. She'd done something that made him sad. And right now she would do anything to change that. 'Sure, if that's what you want.'

He nodded. 'I do.' He put his hand into hers. 'Let's go.'

Things were starting to fall into place in his head. He was starting to almost find a way that he could feel as if he were doing something.

Some of the things that Portia had said today had really hit home. She didn't even realise how many of his buttons she'd pressed. But as he'd watched the sincerity on her face, he'd known she was talking from the heart. It didn't matter she was relating it all to Sofia.

Her feelings were true. Just as his were.

The walls of the attic had felt claustrophobic, as if they were closing in around him. He'd had to get out of there. But he knew exactly who he wanted to get out of there with. She'd revealed a little of the heartache about her sister. As he got to know her just a little more it was clear that Portia Marlowe had just as many chinks in her armour as he had.

For him it was a relief. Portia might be press. But slowly but surely the press walls around her were fading away.

She'd taken less than five minutes to get ready for the beach. He loved that about her. He'd spent days on set waiting six hours for his female co-star to get ready. This was a revelation.

He'd just pulled a different T-shirt on and grabbed a pair of swimming shorts that he'd purchased on one of his trips into the village. He might be Italian—but he didn't do trunks. As far as Javier was concerned they were for competitive swimmers and multimillion-dollar advertisements.

Portia came out with her hair around her shoulders and wearing a hot-pink bikini and matching coverall. It made his heart zing. She looked amazing, and it was clear she was completely unaware of this.

She patted her stomach. 'This is when I'm especially glad we're not in LA right now. A few weeks here, with all the pastries and coffees, makes me lazy. I never want to exercise again.'

'What do you do back home?'

'For exercise?'

He nodded.

She rolled her eyes. 'Same as everyone else. I have a personal trainer. I try not to obsess. You'll know, there's too much of that in Hollywood. Anyone who's bigger than a size two over there is considered overweight. And let's face it—there's history in my family that makes me not go down that road.' She looked sideways at him as he grabbed some water and a few beers from the fridge. 'What do you do?'

He pulled a face. 'Depends entirely on the movie. For the action movie they wanted me to be pure muscle. I'll not pretend. It was hard. Training six hours a day for two months before filming began, and eating six weird tiny meals a day. I was quite irritable. It didn't suit me.'

She smiled. 'Did your co-stars complain about you?'

'Who knows? If I was tense, I took myself out of the way. Filming is full of coffee and donuts and if I wanted to keep my physique on set I had to steer clear of all that. When it's sixteen hours a day it's hard.'

They walked out onto the terrace then down the narrow path. Javier walking ahead and taking her hand down the steep bits. He glanced back as they walked down the path. She'd mentioned something back in the kitchen that made him curious. 'Your sister—Immi—is she well now?'

Portia nodded. 'She is. It took a few years. And I have to admit we all still have the signs tucked away in the back of our minds. Seeing your sister unwell is tough. We all felt as if we'd failed her—especially Mum and Dad. But Miranda, Andie, her twin, took it really badly too.'

Javier looked thoughtful. 'How did she get well again?'

Portia was watching her steps down the steep path. 'She had to be ready. She had to want to get better—and she had to have the right help. Some place that was a good fit for her. My mum and dad tried different therapists, different support groups and doctors. Finally, they found somewhere that specialised entirely on her condition. They were perfect for Immi because that's where all the expertise was.'

Something about her words made him smile. He'd made the right decision. The charity he wanted to start would focus entirely on bipolar disorder. There were various mental health charities and helplines in Italy. There were other helplines for those who were feeling suicidal. But he wanted his charity to specialise and focus entirely on the one disorder that had affected his friend, and still affected his mother. Portia's words just reinforced his decision even more.

The sandy beach was beautiful. Like a forgotten hidden private hideaway. Javier laid their towels on the beach and looked out over the clear azure-blue sea, rippling with tiny peaks of white. In the far, far distance there was a white yacht that looked as if it were moored for fishing.

Portia sagged down onto the beach and put her hands above her head and stretched out. He couldn't help but watch, appreciating her long legs and the look of pure and utter relief on her face. Once she'd finished stretching she turned on her side to face him.

She had no make-up on, there was still a tiny trace of grime in her hair and it made him reach out to wipe it away. He leaned closer. 'Hey, I never told you what my favourite type of exercise is,' he said softly.

She blinked and right before his eyes her pupils widened.

All of a sudden he realised what he'd said. He almost laughed. But he just couldn't do it. Not while he was here with her.

Portia was gradually sneaking her way under all the layers of armour that he had. She asked questions. But not like a reporter. She asked questions like a normal interested human being. He'd kind of forgotten what that felt like.

He knew what he had to do next. He'd finalised his ideas last night and his next steps would take him back to the mainland. But there was still time. Still time to tease out where this connection could take them.

He'd been making plans in his head. Some would need to be firmed up in person, and for that he'd need to go somewhere else. And he knew the perfect person to take with him.

'Is it a secret, or are you going to tell me?' she asked, then lowered her voice to a whisper, 'And is it exercise for one, or for two?'

So she hadn't missed the unintentional innuendo in his words. He actually wished it had been intended. He sat up and stretched his hand out towards her, inviting her to take it.

'My favourite kind of exercise is the entirely natural kind.'

She raised her eyebrows and slid her hand into his. 'Oh?'

He pulled her up towards him, letting her body collide with his, so he could slide his hand down her back to the small hollow where it seemed to fit perfectly.

She snaked her hands around his neck. 'Why do I think that you're teasing me right now?'

'Me?'

She tapped her hands at the backs of his shoulders. 'Yes, you.'

He laughed and lowered his lips so they brushed against her ear. 'Okay, then. My favourite form of exercise—at least, until we're better acquainted—is swimming. How about a race to the buoy out there? You wouldn't come swimming with me the other day.'

It was like two different people in his arms. Her cheeks flushed a little at his hint of something else, then paled instantly at the second suggestion.

She kept her arms tightly around his neck. He turned so they were chest to chest instead of sideways on. She stared out at the distant buoy in sheer unhidden terror. 'That? You want to swim out to *that*?'

Every muscle in her body had tensed against him. He couldn't understand. 'Of course, it's maybe half a mile? It's an easy swim. We can do it together.'

She shook her head fiercely. 'Oh, no. No way. Not me.' Then she glanced at him. 'And not you either. You're not going out there.'

He started laughing. 'Portia, what on earth is wrong?'

She looked at him incredulously. 'What's wrong?' She swept her arm out towards the ocean. 'Look at it. All beautiful and blue. All tempting. All come-and-swim-in-me.'

'Exactly. Let's do it.'

She screwed up her face. 'Not a chance. Do you have any idea what could be out there?'

He pulled back to get a good look at her whole horrified expression. 'No. What?'

She stared back at him. 'Sharks,' she whispered fiercely.

He shook his head. 'You're joking, aren't you?' He couldn't believe it.

'Of course I'm not joking. Every time I see someone swimming in the ocean I hear the *Jaws* theme tune playing in my head. I like the sea. From a distance.'

'But just after we met you were in the sea with me.'

She gulped. 'I wasn't in the sea. Not properly anyway. I'll paddle. But that's it.'

Javier didn't hesitate. He swept Portia up into his arms and started striding towards the ocean.

'Don't you dare! Stop!' she yelled as she thudded her fists on his chest.

He laughed as he walked ankle deep into the waves. 'What about here? Is this where you want me to stop?'

She stopped panicking for a second and looked down. The water was barely around his ankles. 'Don't go any further.'

He smiled and took a few strides further. 'No!' she shrieked.

He stopped again. 'Watch out,' he said. 'If you keep struggling, I might drop you.'

She sucked in a breath and froze.

'How far would you actually go in the water?'

She still looked scared. 'Maybe my knees. Definitely not the chest.'

'Why not?' He couldn't help but be curious.

'Stop laughing at me. I'd never get in the ocean

back home. Sharks are all over LA. I've no idea if there are sharks around here.'

She did look panicked. He shook his head. 'I'm sure there are basking sharks, but none could come this close to shore. And they're quite harmless.'

She squinted at him as the sun's glare fell over her face. 'Do you really swim in LA?'

He nodded. 'Every day. Have done for years.'

She glanced down again warily. 'Well, I'll never go deeper than my knees. I've had a recurring nightmare about sharks for years. I heard that if you punch a shark on the nose it stuns it, and it goes away. And they can come quite close to shore. That's why I'd never wade out to chest height—too dangerous.'

He loved this. He loved that when he stripped back all the parts Portia Marlowe just made him laugh. She made him comfortable. She was fun to be around.

It didn't help that he also loved the way she screwed up her nose and squinted at him in the sun. He loved the way she wasn't obsessed about her weight.

'Would you feel safer if I held you? I thought you wanted to wash the cobwebs out of your hair?'

Her eyes opened wide. 'Oh, yes. That's right. I did.' She pulled a little closer to him as she looked at the clear sea surrounding them.

'Okay, you can take a few more steps, then that's it. You've got to stop.'

'Okay, then.' He couldn't stop smiling as he strode up to his waist. 'How about I just lean you back a little?'

She looked around again and loosened her hands just a little from his neck. 'Okay, but be quick.'

He let his legs bend and kept his hands under her back, so that she floated in the sea and her dark hair fanned out all around her. She stayed like that for a few seconds.

She was beautiful. Like a siren floating in the sea in front of him. That bright pink bikini enhanced all her curves and complemented her light tan. If she started singing any time soon he swore he would just give up and follow her wherever she wanted.

She gave him a signal and he pulled her back up. The water was dripping from her hair and her body. He took a few steps further back.

'What are you doing?'

'Making sure you stay in my arms.'

She gave him a curious stare, then wrapped her arms back around his neck and then her legs around his waist. 'Now, why would you want to do that?'

He didn't answer straight away. He wasn't entirely sure of the answer he could give. Instead he asked what was forefront on his mind. 'I need to do some business tomorrow. It means I have to go to Naples. Would you like to come with me? The business won't take long, and I love the opera in Naples. I've checked and *Le Nozze di Figaro* is showing at Teatro di San Carlo.' He gave her a wink. 'I might even know where you can find a dress you can wear.'

She gave a gasp and stared at him. 'You honestly think I should wear one of Sofia's dresses?'

He leaned back into the water. 'Why not? You'll look every bit as elegant in them as she did.'

He could tell she was a bit embarrassed, but also happy with the compliment.

'Hey, isn't it time you got me out of this water?'

Javier felt a little swell in his chest. The water droplets left on her body were virtually glistening in the sun. The feel of her body against his was having all the natural effects it should. He'd kind of hoped wading deeper, where the water might be colder, would have helped—but the fire inside was too strong. A few days of virtually not speaking had done nothing to cool the heat between them—instead it seemed to only have intensified the burn. Her dark hair and gleaming dark eyes were enticing him in ways he hadn't felt in years.

He tightened his grip on her hips. 'Maybe I just want to take you deeper into the ocean. Maybe I need some kind of persuasion not to.'

She lowered her gaze playfully. 'Oh, I think I can find a way to entice you.'

His pulse soared. 'How?'

She licked her lips and tilted her head to one side. Her lips met his. The smouldering fire ignited like a shooting firework. Her smooth lips moved over his with expert grace, coaxing, teasing and sending all sane thoughts floating off into the ocean around them.

And he was well and truly enticed.

CHAPTER SIX

SHE WAS NERVOUS. Her stomach had danced in knots all day. Last night they'd come up from the beach and drunk wine together in the painted drawing room by candlelight.

It was probably the most romantic setting in the world, and she wondered how often Sofia had sat in there with Ludano. Javier had kissed her as if she were the only woman on the planet and for a few hours she'd forgotten about everything else.

She'd forgotten about the job she didn't want any more.

She'd forgotten about being the oldest sister left on the shelf.

She'd forgotten about her experience of love in Hollywood.

She'd forgotten about all her curiosity about Javier.

And she'd forgotten about figuring out what to do with her life.

For that little bubble of time it had been just him, and her. And it had felt almost perfect.

Today had felt unreal. Javier had finished putting the coloured panes in the conservatory. She'd tidied out a bit more of the attic, labelling boxes that Posy would need to search through. It had been fortuitous. She'd found another trunk full of shoes and found a pair that would match the red dress perfectly. Javier had disappeared into the village for a while to arrange transport for them to the ferry and she'd packed her overnight clothes and evening dress in a light bag.

It was afternoon before they took the ferry to the mainland. As soon as they neared the Italian coastline her phone started to ping. She pulled it from her bag. Six voicemails. A few hundred emails. And numerous text messages.

Javier must have noticed the pained expression on her face. 'I'm not even looking at mine. There's someone I need to phone to finalise our meeting when we reach Naples—but that's it. Everything else can wait.'

She stared at him for a second. He seemed relaxed. He seemed sure. Almost as if he'd made up his mind about something.

She wished she could make her mind up about things. Maybe making a decision would make her feel better?

'Is there anyone you really need to call?' he pressed. 'Do you think any of it is an emergency?'

She had a quick scroll. There were a few messages from her sisters. She texted back some quick replies. Everything else seemed safe to ignore. 'No, I guess there isn't.' She put her phone on silent and stuffed it back in her bag.

She took a deep breath and leaned back against the railing of the ferry. If Javier Russo could ignore his phone, then she could too. The ferry was taking its time docking. She nudged Javier. 'Look around us. What do you notice?'

He glanced from side to side and frowned. 'I don't know. What is it?'

She gave him a smile. 'What's different about here, and what happens in L'Isola dei Fiori?'

He seemed puzzled but looked around again.

After a few seconds he shook his head and turned back. 'Okay, you've got me. Is this a trick question?'

She laughed. 'No, silly. The phones. Most of the people on the ferry are all currently staring at their phones. We don't see that in L'Isola dei Fiori. People still sit at dinner tables and talk to each other. Have conversations. I'm beginning to think that humans are losing the art of conversation because we spend so much time with our heads in our phones. Weren't you twitchy the first few days you arrived? You get so used to having the world at your fingertips you forget how to manage without it.'

He leaned closer to her and smiled. 'Maybe these people should consider other distractions?' Something had definitely changed in Javier. He'd said he had some business to do but he also seemed more positive, more enthusiastic. The twinkle in his eyes that had dulled for a few days was definitely back.

His words sent a little shot of heat through her veins. She couldn't help but smile. 'Watch out, there are children about. Some distractions aren't for public viewing.'

'You think?' Before she got a chance to reply he lowered his lips onto hers. It wasn't a soft kiss. It was purposeful. As if he seemed certain of what he was doing. It was easy to put her hand up and run it through his short dark hair.

Something twigged inside her. A sense of belonging. Something she hadn't ever felt before.

As if, even though her rational brain told her otherwise, this seemed like the right time, in the right place with the right person.

Almost as if he were hers.

Something about that terrified her. Her stomach flip-flopped but her heart was practically swelling in her chest. Now, she got what Andie felt. She just wasn't entirely sure if this could all be real.

The ferry gave a jerk as it finally moored into place. They laughed as their heads clashed and Javier threaded his fingers with hers as he carried their bags from the ferry terminal.

It was busy here. There was instantly a buzz in the air that wasn't present in the more sedate

L'Isola dei Fiori. And more people meant more chance of recognition. Not for her, but for him. Javier was Italy's biggest ever film star.

As they exited the terminal she saw a few curious glances. If they'd been in an airport she was sure that phones would have been whipped out and a million pictures snapped. But no one would expect Javier Russo to be coming off the ferry from the little-known kingdom of L'Isola dei Fiori.

He led her towards some waiting cars. He gave a nod to a uniformed chauffeur outside a long black limousine and threw their bags in the boot as the chauffeur opened the door for her. As the door closed behind her, Portia was happy to hide behind the black tinted glass.

She was starting to feel self-conscious. In Los Angeles she always took care of her appearance when she was out and about. Lots of people recognised her from the TV show and it would be bad publicity to be snapped looking frumpy and tired.

She hadn't even thought about it this morning. Even though she had the evening dress in her bag, she'd thrown on a pair of jeans, tied up her hair and not bothered with make-up. Her only partial saving grace was the sunglasses she was wearing.

'What's wrong?' Javier slid his hand over hers.

'Nothing.' She tried to push the self-conscious thoughts from her head. No one cared what she looked like. No one knew who she was.

He gave her thigh a squeeze. 'Have you visited Naples before?'

She shook her head. 'No. Never.'

His brow furrowed. 'If I'd planned ahead we could have stayed longer—done a tour of the city.' She could see him biting his lip. 'Do you want to see if we can stay an extra day?'

She shook her head. 'No, it's fine. To be honest I've been enjoying the sanctuary of Villa Rosa. I can't stay there forever and it's been a long time since I had a proper holiday. I'm learning that I can actually live without social media, and it's a revelation.'

His face broke into a broad smile. 'It is, isn't it? There's something nice about not living at such a frantic pace.' He rested back against the leather seats. 'Have you been to the opera before?'

She shook her head. 'Never. We weren't an opera kind of family. My parents—as you know—were Shakespeare nuts. We spent our lives seeing every production of Shakespeare. Then, when Posy was young she loved musicals. I've seen every one of those until they were imprinted in my brain. And the last fifteen years, it's been constant ballet. I've spent a lot of time sitting in a theatre—just never at an opera.'

He gave a nod. 'I can't wait until we get there. Teatro di San Carlo is magnificent. Like something from a bygone age. You'll love it.'

She smiled back nervously. 'I hope so.' She looked out of the window at the city flashing past outside. 'Where are we going to stay?'

'I've booked a suite at one of the hotels for the night. I've stayed there before. If you're hungry we can order some room service before we head out to the opera.'

She gave a nod and took a deep breath as she watched out of the window. Javier's hand stayed over hers. Naples passed by quickly. A suite.

What did that mean? After what had happened last night between them, she couldn't help but think about what would come next. A suite in a luxury hotel somehow felt like the next step on the horizon. Nervous excitement bubbled in her stomach. It was like being a teenager all over again.

The limousine pulled up outside a grand-looking hotel. Everything was perfection. The foyer was all exquisite cream marble. They were shown to a private lift that took them up to the twenty-fifth floor.

As the elevator doors slid open Portia let out a gasp. The suite was huge, with spectacular floor-to-ceiling glass doors looking out over the Bay of Naples.

Javier tipped the concierge and took their bags, walking across the room and pulling one of the doors open, letting the warm air flood in.

He walked outside onto the balcony, resting his hands on the railing, and sucked in a deep breath. He gave her a smile. 'It doesn't quite have the tranquillity of Villa Rosa, but this place comes a close second for me.' He waved his hand downwards. 'On one side of the suite you can watch the buzz of the city, from the other you have this, the beautiful bay.'

She stood alongside him and admired the view. Vesuvius was in the distance, along with the coastline of Sorrento and isle of Capri. Underneath them was a whole array of million-dollar yachts.

She laid her head on his shoulder. 'I often wonder how long it will be before Vesuvius erupts again. I visited Pompeii once with my family. It was like stepping back in time. Everything about it felt so real. From the stepping stones, to the mosaics, and the amphitheatre.'

He nodded. 'We should go there again some day.'

Her mouth dried. That almost sounded like a plan. Something for the future. She wasn't quite sure how to reply.

Javier turned back towards her. 'I have a business meeting I need to attend.' He hesitated then pointed inside the suite. 'You're welcome to take any of the rooms, or you can share mine. And I'll order some room service while you get ready. Teatro di San Carlo is only five minutes from here.'

She gave a little nod. He seemed a little nervous too; he hadn't made the assumption she'd be sharing his room—that was up to her.

He bent down and brushed a kiss on her cheek. 'I'll see you in a couple of hours.'

She gave a nod as he disappeared back out of the door of the suite. Portia turned and faced the Bay of Naples again. She wasn't quite sure what the night would hold, but she couldn't wait to find out.

The meeting went well. Things were finally falling into place in his brain. He'd recognised something in the last few days. Aldo had left a message saying he wanted to talk.

Talk. It was the common theme for people with bipolar disorder who were feeling suicidal. Javier had done his research. There was no specific charity in Italy for people who had bipolar disorder. One of his biggest ambitions was awareness raising. There could be other families out there watching a loved one deteriorate and not recognising the signs. Not recognising the condition. And for people already diagnosed and experiencing the extreme mood swings that could come with bipolar disorder there would be somewhere they could call. A safe place when they were struggling. How many people could be helped if they had a place they could call when they felt at their lowest? Could it have helped Aldo?

He'd never really know. But it made him feel as if he were doing *something.* Something that might help others who felt the same way.

The charity was his starting point. He had more than enough money to fund this. He just had to make the right connections to make sure this could be set up safely, and well. And that was exactly what he'd been doing today.

He glanced at his watch. The details had taken longer than expected. He'd need to be quick to get ready for the opera. When the doors of the lift opened, he could see signs of Portia throughout the suite. A coffee cup. A plate of pastries. Her computer sitting on the desk.

Music was playing in one of the other rooms.

His heart sank a little as he walked through to the main room and then stopped. Her bag was lying in the corner of his room. She might be taking time to get ready in another room, but it looked as if it was her intention to sleep here.

His heart gave a lurch in his chest. He could almost feel the blood quicken around his body. He strode into the bathroom and turned on the shower. His tuxedo was hanging in the wardrobe and the champagne that he'd ordered was sitting chilling in a bucket of ice.

It didn't take him long to shower, shave and change. He carried the ice bucket and glasses out into the main room just as the music in the other room was turned off.

The sun was beginning to set outside, filling the bay with streaks of orange and red. Javier glanced at his watch. They only had a little time before they would need to leave for the opera. Just as he thought about calling her, Portia opened the door from the other room.

He could tell she was nervous. She was taking tentative steps and had one hand on her stomach. The off-the-shoulder long red dress was stunning; it both hugged and complemented her curves, dipping slightly at the front. Her hair was curled, cascading over one shoulder. She had no jewellery on. She didn't need any. Instead, she wore long black gloves, completing her look of elegance.

'Wow,' was all he could say.

She looked over her shoulder as if he were talking to someone else, then her face broke into a wide smile. 'You think it will do?'

He popped the cork on the champagne and filled the two glasses, holding one out towards her. 'I think…' he paused '…that you're perfect.'

She was wearing make-up now. Black kohl around her eyes and red lips to match her dress. Her hand shook as she took the glass from him. 'I am?'

He nodded as he placed one hand at her hip. 'You are.'

The nervousness started to fall away from her face. Her dark eyes swept up and down him. 'You don't scrub up too badly yourself.' She winked at him. 'You should try and get a part that means you wear a tux in a film.' She sipped her champagne as she smiled. He got the hint about the world's most famous spy instantly.

He laughed. 'I think you'll find that particular part is quintessentially English.' He did his best impression of an English accent.

Portia laughed too. 'I've always thought that was a flaw.' She waved her champagne glass. 'They need to broaden their horizons. They're missing out on some prime candidates for the role.'

He guided her over towards the view of Naples bay again. She let out a little sigh. 'It's like someone planned this night perfectly.' She held out her hand. 'A stunning dress, a wonderful view, a luxurious hotel…' she turned and rested her hand on the front of his tux '…a handsome man and then…opera. What more could a girl want?'

She tilted her chin up towards him. 'What more could she want indeed?' he whispered as he bent to kiss her. He could taste the champagne on her soft, tempting lips. Her body turned towards his and it was easy to slide his hand down her back and press his hips against hers. Her perfume wound its way around him, pulling him in like the music of a snake charmer.

Nothing felt wrong. Everything felt right. For the first time since Aldo had died Javier finally had some peace. He could finally contemplate a future. And he knew exactly who he wanted to contemplate it with. Her breath was quickening, their kisses becoming more fevered, and he reluctantly pulled his lips from hers and pressed his forehead against hers.

'Ms Marlowe?' he said hoarsely.

She looked up through thick lashes. 'Yes?' Her voice was shaking.

He held out his hand to take her gloved one. 'Let me introduce you to the magic of opera. Let me introduce you to *The Marriage of Figaro*.'

It was as if she were in her own movie.

She was the heroine. And he was the hero.

In some ways she felt as if it were all unreal. As if at any moment she'd wake up from this wonderful dream.

The limousine whisked them to the Teatro di San Carlo. As soon as they stepped outside it was like being on the red carpet. Javier was recognised instantly. She could feel the electricity in the air around them. His hand stayed firmly at her back.

Cameras flashed intermittently. Javier shook hands with people and charmed his way along the row of staff who were standing outside the opera house.

As soon as they stepped inside her nerves increased. There were many hushed voices and glances in their direction. What a fool. She hadn't given this enough thought.

She'd got used to the anonymity of L'Isola dei Fiori. Of not looking over her shoulder and worrying about what she looked like. It was odd. The thought had flitted through her mind when they were on the ferry. But since they'd arrived in the hotel it had been like their own private world, and when she'd stepped outside the room and seen Javier's face, all she'd been able to think about was him and her.

Another glass of champagne was placed in her hand and she gathered Sofia's dress in one hand as they walked up the stairs.

Walking into the *teatro* was like entering another world.

It was breathtaking. The whole theatre was circular, set around the large stage. Red plush seats filled the stalls and sweeping around the walls were five tiers of individual boxes. White and gold gilt decorated the walls with sweeping red velvet curtains at each of the boxes.

Javier smiled at her and led her up a set of private stairs. A staff member held the door open for her and she stepped inside. And then stopped.

They were directly facing the stage. The box had large sumptuous seats and gold gilt decoration all around. 'What is this?' she whispered.

He smiled. 'We're in the royal box.'

'The what?' It was almost as if the air had been sucked from her chest. Maybe this dress was tighter than she thought.

He gestured to her to sit down. The chair was almost like a throne, possibly the grandest chair she'd ever seen. She perched gingerly on the edge while an amused Javier watched. More champagne was waiting for them in the box along with strawberries. 'I thought you might be hungry.' he said with a shrug. Javier settled next to her as the lights started to dim around them.

'Do you know the story of *The Marriage of Figaro*?'

She nodded. 'I've never seen it though.'

He smiled and rested back in his chair as he clasped her hand. 'Then sit back and enjoy, let the magic begin.'

From the first beat of the music it was like a spell being weaved around her. Figaro, Susanna and the Count gripped her attention. Every one of Mozart's notes, every harmony, every element of comedy had her enthralled. The music from the opera filled every part of the huge theatre, reverberating around them.

In the dark of the theatre their box seemed ultimately private. So when Javier nuzzled at her neck she didn't object. He fed her strawberries, which trickled down her chin. The champagne made her hiccup, which set her off in a fit of giggles.

And he didn't let go of her hand the whole night.

She stopped worrying about her work and her

life in Hollywood. Javier only had eyes for her. His attention was mesmerising. They whispered to each other. They kissed. She'd never been so connected.

Her heart was swelling so much it felt as though it would fill her chest. When the last beat of music had finished she leapt to her feet and applauded as loudly as she could.

Javier was at her side. 'Did you like it?'

She couldn't hold back the enthusiasm that was bubbling inside. She threw her arms around his neck. 'I didn't like it, I loved it.'

He looked so amused, but she felt safe around him, assured in his arms. That glint in his eye sent little shockwaves all around her body. No one had ever made her feel like this. No one had ever made her feel so special, and so loved.

She forgot about everyone else around them as they walked hand in hand to the limousine. She only had eyes for Javier. And it seemed he only had eyes for her.

By the time they'd reached the hotel she was breathless with anticipation.

The journey in the lift only took a few seconds and she held her breath the whole way.

Javier was quiet. Maybe he was feeling the same way. As the doors slid open she could see candles flickering all around the suite. Gentle music was playing in the background. It was magical.

But for some reason her feet couldn't move.

Javier stepped out of the lift and turned and held his hand out towards her. 'Ms Marlowe…' he bowed before her '…will you be my guest?'

Every part of her was trembling. But it wasn't nerves. It was excitement.

She'd never wanted anything more.

'I'd love to,' she answered as she put her hand in his.

Javier pulled her up against him. They'd never danced together before and this felt exactly how it should.

She slid her arms up to his shoulders and pressed her body against his, moving in time with the music. Javier's mouth trailed kisses down the side of her face and along her shoulder and neck.

His touch so light, it was like butterfly wings against her skin.

Her skin was on fire. Every sense aching for his touch. His fingers traced a line down her closed eyes, past her mouth and over the delicate skin at her decoupage, stopping tantalisingly at the mound of her breasts. He moved it across her chest and down the length of one arm, spinning her around so she had her back to him and peeling her glove, oh, so slowly, so temptingly down her arm. It was like being part of an exotic and extremely private striptease. The next glove followed just as slowly. She could feel the planes of his chest and abdomen pressed against her back. She sucked in a breath as his hand slid between their bodies and rested in the arch between her shoulder blades. The noise of the slide of the zipper was achingly teasing. As the pressure of the dress released around her, she spun around, letting it fall on the floor at her feet and leaving her standing in only her underwear in front of him.

She didn't feel embarrassed. She didn't feel exposed. She just lifted her hands and started slowly pulling his bow tie apart. He stood still, not moving as she took charge. Instead, she relished him watching the candlelight dance over her body as she slowly undid each button on his shirt. Once she'd pulled it apart she slid her hands over the planes of his chest as he let out a groan. He pulled her bare breasts against his now bare chest.

'Do you know what you're doing to me, Portia Marlowe?'

She licked her lips as she lowered her gaze. 'Pretty much the same as you're doing to me, Mr Russo. How about we see where this takes us?'

She let out a whimper as his hands slid over the curves of her bottom. 'Let's see indeed,' he groaned as he lowered her to the floor.

CHAPTER SEVEN

HE WOKE UP with the sheets tangled around him and her bare body pressed against his.

In previous circumstances he'd always known there would be an end point in the relationship. He'd never been sworn on forever.

But with Portia he just couldn't picture how things would come to a natural end.

He didn't want to.

She smiled as she turned around, still sleeping, and reached out to press her head against his chest. He ran his fingertip down her nose. 'Hey, sleepyhead. We need to wake up at some point. We need to get back to our own private paradise.'

She let out a groan, still not opening her eyes. 'I like the sound of that.'

But she wasn't finished. She stretched, then swung one leg over his body, sitting astride him and brushing her lips against his. 'I love Villa

Rosa, but I'm kind of liking it here too. Why don't we stay another night? Do a tour of the city like you said?'

He hesitated, trying to find the words. But they didn't come quickly enough. His mind was blank. Everything had gone well yesterday. But he was anxious to finish at Villa Rosa and get back to the real world. Get back to where he felt he could make a difference. He just hadn't had a chance to talk to Portia about it yet.

'How about we save that for another day? I'd like to finish up at Villa Rosa first.'

She frowned and sat back, placing her palms flat on his chest. Even though this was a little awkward, part of him loved that she wasn't embarrassed by their nakedness. She looked the tiniest bit hurt. 'Oh, okay, then.'

She sighed and swung her leg back from his body and stepped down onto the floor. She walked over to the wardrobe and pulled it open, reaching for one of the white luxury dressing gowns that hung inside. She wrapped it around herself and turned around. 'I think you should order me some coffee. It's time for you to tell me what's going on.'

He could tell by the tone of her voice that he wouldn't be able to brush her off with any made-up tales. And he didn't want to do that anyway.

They'd got this close. Maybe it was time to finally share the secret that had been eating away at him since he'd got the phone call to say that Aldo was dead.

It was surprising how quickly room service could arrive. Within ten minutes they were sitting on either side of a table with an array of food in front of them. Portia pulled one leg up onto the chair, revealing her bare knee as she reached for a croissant and tore it apart. Her dark curls from last night tumbled around her face. Not a trace of make-up was left.

He poured the coffee and left it black.

Portia didn't speak, she just studied him with her dark brown eyes.

'You know how we spoke about the funeral I went to just before the awards ceremony?'

She nodded. 'It was a friend, wasn't it? I just

assumed he'd died of cancer or something similar. You never really told me much about it.'

He nodded. 'I know. I never told anyone much about it.'

She narrowed her gaze. 'Okay, why?'

He felt his voice start to shake. 'Aldo was my oldest friend. I'd known him forever. He still lived in the village my mother's family came from. Aldo didn't die from cancer.'

She set down her coffee cup. 'What did he die from?'

Javier's eyes went to the bay, sweeping around the beauty of the view and glistening sea. 'Aldo committed suicide.'

Saying the words out loud was so harsh. It was like an admission of reality. The thing he really didn't want to talk about at all—but was trying to find a way to deal with.

'Oh.' Portia pressed her lips together. She was still studying him intently. 'I'm really sorry to hear that.' She waited a few seconds and then added, 'Had he been unwell?'

Bile rose in the back of his throat. There was an ache in his stomach. A real, physical ache. A gust of wind blew in through the open doors, carrying the aroma of all the food on the table, and he almost retched. Javier pushed his chair back from the table.

As he looked down he saw the goosebumps appear on his skin. 'Yes—but I didn't know it.' He ran his fingers through his hair. 'I didn't recognise the signs.' He shook his head. 'I wasn't there to recognise the signs.'

Portia spoke quietly. 'What do you mean?'

Javier's grey eyes met hers, pain etched through them. 'Aldo had bipolar disorder—just like my mother has.'

Portia's eyes widened. 'Oh.'

He shook his head. 'I spent my life around someone with bipolar disorder. If anyone should have recognised it—it should have been me. But I wasn't there. I didn't see enough of Aldo. I knew he was down. I knew he was depressed—but I thought that seemed like part of the grieving process after the breakdown of his marriage.'

'And it was more than that?'

Javier nodded. 'Yes. His sister told me later about the mood swings. The sleeplessness. The irritability. The erratic behaviour.' He leaned forward and put his head in his hands. 'All things I could have recognised.'

'And if you had—would you have been able to help?'

Javier threw up his hands in frustration. 'Of course I would have. I could have got him to see a specialist doctor, a therapist that could have helped with his condition.'

She gave her head a little shake. 'This isn't your fault, Javier. You weren't here. You were working.'

Javier clenched his fists. 'I know that. But still…'

Javier looked up and met her gaze. Those dark brown eyes were fixed on his. No judgement. No blame. His voice broke. 'There's more.'

Portia leaned across the table and squeezed his hand. 'What?'

He let out a long slow breath.

'I hadn't been good at keeping in touch. I'd called. I'd emailed. But we hadn't physically seen each other for seventeen months.' He shook his head and bowed it. 'That was far too long. Far too long for someone I'd known that long.'

Portia still had her hand over his. She stopped squeezing and started moving her thumb in little circles over his knuckles. 'But that happens with friends. Even the best of friends. I have friends from school that I only ever get to see every five years or so, and we just pick up from where we left off. Time doesn't matter to us. We're all leading our own lives.' Her hand came up and touched his cheek. 'But they're the kind of friends—almost like sisters—that I know if I picked up the phone to them in the middle of the night and told them I was in trouble, they'd drop everything to help me. And I would them.'

He could see the sincerity on her face. She absolutely meant it. Portia Marlowe was a much better friend than he'd ever been.

He snatched his hand back and stalked out to the balcony, putting his arms on the railing and stretching down, closing his eyes and willing the Bay winds to sweep away his conscience and regrets.

'Javier?' Portia stood beside him in her dressing gown, worry etched across her face. Her voice was quiet. 'What is it?'

She knew there was so much more to this. He couldn't pretend any more.

He started to shake. 'It was my fault, Portia. Mine. I was away—filming in the Arabian Desert. It was a terrible location. No phone signals. Sixteen-hour days on set. And even as I say that out loud I know exactly what a pathetic excuse that is.' His voice was getting louder. He couldn't help himself. He was so wrapped up in the emotion that he couldn't stop. 'He phoned me, Portia. He phoned me and left me a message saying he really needed to talk. And do you know what I did? I got back to the trailer, couldn't get a signal and fell asleep. *I fell asleep!*'

Portia had pulled back, her eyes wide. But she stood her ground next to him as her hair was blown around her face.

'What kind of friend am I? My best friend calls—tells me he needs me. And I'm too busy—too tired to call back. I was the last person Aldo called before he killed himself.' He thudded his hands down on the railing.

His breaths were coming in short, sharp bursts. He could feel his heart thudding against his chest.

There was a flicker to his left. Someone standing on the balcony of the neighbouring suite; a man also stood looking out over the bay.

Portia didn't speak. She just took one of his hands and pulled him back indoors. She pushed him firmly down onto one of the large armchairs and settled on his lap.

She wrapped her arms around his neck and dipped her head next to his ear. 'Don't, Javier. Don't do this to yourself. Don't blame yourself because you didn't answer the phone on one occasion. You have no idea if it would have made a difference or not. How could you? If you had spoken to him, and he'd still done it, would you feel better or worse?'

He was numb. But Portia was sitting in his lap, putting her cheek against his and letting the heat from her body reach through the robe towards him.

His throat was completely dry. Her fingers stroked through his hair. She was trying to offer some modicum of comfort.

His voice was throaty. 'He wanted to talk, Portia. That's what he said. He just wanted to talk.'

She gave her head the smallest shake. 'But you still don't know. You had no idea your friend was unwell. If you had done—I'm sure you would have called him straight away.' She closed her eyes for a second. 'We all have points in our lives where we'd like to turn the clock back and take different steps. But that doesn't always mean we've done something wrong.' Her hand was still on his face. 'What about his mum and dad? His sister? How are they doing?'

'I try and speak to them every week. I don't think his mum or dad will ever get over it. How do you do that? How does a parent get over losing a child?'

'And they didn't know either?'

He shook his head. 'That's just it. They didn't recognise the signs. He'd lost weight. He'd apparently mentioned he had trouble sleeping. His moods were erratic.'

She held out her hands. 'And because of your experience with your mother, you think you would have put the pieces together?'

He gave the briefest of nods. His emotions were bubbling beneath the surface. He'd never really spoken to anyone about all this before. He'd never really shared like this. It didn't matter that there was still that tiny voice in the back of his brain, telling him that Portia was a reporter. The woman he'd come to know in the last few days hadn't shown any cut-throat tactics that he'd seen in his childhood. None of the deviousness. None of the manipulative behaviour. The Portia Marlowe he knew had a good and honest heart.

She was nodding slowly as she looked out over the bay. 'So what is it that you want to do here?'

'You mentioned your sister needed specialist help. I want to do that for Aldo's condition—for bipolar disorder. The meeting yesterday—it was with a potential director for the charity I want to set up. I want to set up a helpline. I want to raise awareness of the signs of the condition. I want to organise support groups for those that need it—and specialist help.'

She gave a serious nod. 'That's a huge undertaking.'

'I know. But it's something I need to do. The

money is easy—I have the money. I have more money than I can actually spend. I just need to be sure that I set up things to work well.'

Portia looked serious. 'It could be a minefield. You have to be prepared for anything.' She paused for a second. 'People will wonder why Javier Russo is so interested in bipolar disorder. You'll have to be prepared for the press you might get.'

'I know.'

He could see her concentrating. 'What about your mum?'

He nodded. 'She's well right now. She hasn't worked as a model in years. Times have changed. She's ready to talk about her mental health condition.'

He was overwhelmed by how understanding Portia was being. She was taking what he was saying seriously. She hadn't let him think—even for the briefest second—that she was disappointed he hadn't returned the call to Aldo straight away. She'd been kind. She'd been rational. And she'd shown him affection and love.

'Thank you,' he whispered.

She looked surprised. 'For what?'

'For being you.'

A soft smile appeared on her lips. 'Why would I be anyone else?' She leaned forward and dropped a gentle kiss on his forehead, her hair brushing against his face. 'You're a good man, Javier. I'm sorry about your friend—really I am. And I understand you wanting to look out for his family.' She slid her hand under his dressing gown and placed it over his heart. 'But you have to look out for yourself too. I get that you want to take some time. I think you're right to stop working so hard. But you need to think carefully about the next steps.'

Javier breathed slowly. It was as if a whole weight had been lifted from his shoulders. He'd shared. He'd said the words out loud that had haunted him for the last few months.

Did fate really put people in your path?

He looked up at the pale blue sky above and smiled. He'd come to Villa Rosa for solitude. For quiet. And instead he'd met Portia Marlowe. With her tumbling curls, perfect English accent and chocolate-brown eyes she'd taken him by surprise. Her intuitive questions. Her feisty attitude. Her laugh. The sometimes suggestive twinkle in her eyes. But most of all her good heart.

Slowly but surely, Portia had burrowed her way under his skin and into his own heart.

The gorgeous woman in his arms right now laughed as her stomach growled loudly. 'Oh, no! That's what happens when you distract me from breakfast.'

She walked back inside for a second, grabbed an apple then walked back out to his side. She looked back over the Bay of Naples and gave a little sigh. 'It's so beautiful here.'

Javier put his hands on her waist. The electric-blue bay was buzzing with activity. White million-dollar yachts and cruise ships bobbed beneath them. The area around the bay was packed with tourists, visiting the shops and heading in towards the city. The distant peak of Vesuvius looked crested in purple this morning with a white cloud misting around it. For lots of people this would be paradise.

Portia waved back in towards the suite. 'And this place is sumptuous. Won't you be sorry to go back to our crumbling Villa Rosa with its antiquated plumbing, dust-filled attics and barely functioning kitchen?'

He bent his head and whispered in her ear. 'Absolutely not. I can't wait.'

She twirled in his arms to face him. 'Really, why?'

'Because Villa Rosa brought me you.'

And he met her lips with his own and they forgot all about breakfast.

Any minute now she was going to wake up and discover this had all been some kind of wistful dream.

Even now it felt too *good* to be a dream.

When Javier had told her about his friend the anguish on his face had been heartbreaking. He truly believed he could have done something differently. The fact he hadn't returned the call straight away would probably haunt him for the rest of his life.

But she loved the fact he was trying to turn something tragic into something positive. Her stomach gave an uncomfortable twist. If she'd come here looking for a story—this was it. And depending on the mood of the press it could be spun either way. In one headline Javier Russo would be the tragic school friend of a man who'd committed suicide and was now trying to start a charity to help others with the same condition. In another, he would be the villain, the heartless Hollywood star who'd ignored the call of a suicidal friend.

But she didn't want a story any more.

She didn't want any of it any more.

All she wanted was Javier. The man who made her blood sizzle just by saying her name with his Italian accent. The man who could entice her to cross a room with one look. The man whose touch she would never tire of.

She wanted to help him. She wanted to support him.

She'd thought leaving Hollywood was a curse—instead it was a blessing. She'd had a chance to connect with someone who made her feel whole. Who made her feel complete.

She hadn't had a chance yet to tell him about her job. Or lack of it.

She'd toyed with the idea of just sending an email to her boss and quitting. But Portia wasn't that kind of girl. She'd meet her boss, have that conversation and walk out of the room with her dignity and pride intact.

She was professional enough to know she didn't want a bad reputation to follow her.

When she got back she would have to pack up her apartment and look for somewhere less expensive to stay. But she didn't care any more. Holly Payne could be the star at Entertainment Buzz TV. Her heart just wasn't in it any more.

Javier's hand stayed intertwined with hers on the car journey back through Naples and then on the ferry back to L'Isola dei Fiori. They talked through his plans for the phone line and she took some notes on questions he needed to ask. His phone rang a few times on the way back. Each time he took it from his pocket, checked it and put it away again.

'You don't want to take it?'

Javier shook his head firmly. 'No. I don't. It's my agent. I think he and I will be parting company soon.'

'You do?'

'I do. Let's just say it's time.'

She licked her lips and looked out at the coastline of L'Isola dei Fiori as the boat moved to dock. 'So, when are you due back home?' Asking the question made her a little nervous. It felt like putting a sign above her head saying, *Do any future plans include me?*

'Home? Oh, you mean Hollywood? That's not really home. I have a house in the hills and a house down in Malibu on the beach.'

'You have an original Malibu beach house?'

'And guess who helped me remodel?'

She laughed. 'Uncle Vinnie?'

'Yep. Uncle Vinnie. And guess what? He was the boss. I had to follow all his instructions.'

'Wow. I'd love to meet Uncle Vinnie. I bet he keeps you on your toes.'

'Oh, he does. He'd love you. Once he hears your accent you'll have him in the palm of your hand.'

A warm feeling spread across her chest. Javier said those words so easily—as if he was assuming she would meet his family.

He flung his arm around her shoulders as they disembarked the ferry. 'I also have a house at Lake Como. You should come and see that some time. I think you'd like it.'

Her footsteps faltered. '*The* Lake Como?'

He gave her an amused smile. 'Is there any other?'

'So, you're next door to George Clooney?'

He didn't miss a beat. 'Almost.'

It was as if someone had just sprinkled fairy dust over her. She'd spent the last few days thinking of Javier Russo, the man—the person. Because that was what he was to her. But it was Javier Russo the movie star that owned houses in the Hollywood Hills, Santa Monica beach and Lake Como.

Their time in Villa Rosa had been blissful. Private. The three weeks would be over soon. Could the connection they'd made here survive in the real world?

Just thinking about it made her stomach flip-flop.

Right now she wanted to direct her own movie. One where she pressed a button and let time stop all around them. Not so much a *Groundhog Day* as a Groundhog Three Weeks. They could live in their own private bubble in the pink villa and let the rest of the world pass them by. If only.

Javier led her into one of the fishmongers at the port. 'Will we grab something for dinner?'

'Sure.' They picked up some fish, some vegetables and new potatoes. Then, they added some wine and took a taxi back to the villa.

This time, when Portia turned the old key in the lock and stepped inside the villa had a different feel.

When she'd done this first time around, she'd been sad, sensing the air of neglect and disrepair around her. Walking through the villa had almost made her feel like a ghost.

This time the air around her almost hummed. Javier was by her side, striding through to the kitchen to deposit their food. Now, she felt a sense of belonging. She wandered through to the painted drawing room. The plaster had dried in a long white crack snaking up the pale blue and mauve sky. The rest of the walls had been skimmed smoothly, ready for painting.

Javier appeared at her side again, sliding his arm around her waist. 'It's beautiful,' she sighed. 'Or at least it will be again once it's painted.' She tilted her chin up towards him. 'You've done a really good job.'

'Why thank you, madam.' He kissed her lips and her hand automatically went to his head, running through his hair and holding his lips on hers.

A sweep of anxious desperation that she hated flooded through her. She just honestly didn't want this time to end.

But it seemed neither did Javier, because he swept one hand under her legs and held her in his arms. His lips touched her ear. 'Your room, or mine?' he whispered.

CHAPTER EIGHT

SHE WAS TEMPTED to skip into the village the next morning, but instead she was happy to walk with Javier's arm around her shoulders. They parted at the top of the street. Javier had decided to buy something special at the fishmonger's for dinner tonight.

There was a crowd outside the newsagents and several faces turned as she approached, scowling at her and murmuring under their breath.

She almost didn't go any further, but one of them moved just enough for her to glimpse the billboard outside the newsagent and let her catch a glance at the headline and photo on the board. A flash of pink caught her attention. An achingly familiar pink bikini.

Her feet moved automatically. She shoved her way through the crowd and picked up the paper at the top of the pile.

She had no idea what the headline said but she could understand the photos—after all a picture spoke a thousand words. They were all of her, entwined around Javier. One from the private beach—he was holding her in the water and she had her legs and arms wrapped around him like some kind of limpet. The next was in the restaurant at the port, the third at the opera in Naples with her wearing Sofia's red dress and the final one—the killer—was of the two of them wearing hotel bathrobes and standing on the balcony of the hotel in Naples.

She couldn't speak. Her mouth was dry. Who on earth had taken these pictures? And what did the story say?

She walked numbly into the Internet café and sat down at one of the computers. She winced as she searched for her own name and Javier's.

If she'd thought Holly had caused an Internet explosion a few weeks ago, then she and Javier had caused an Internet meltdown. At least in the US and in Italy.

But as she started to read the hairs on her arms stood on end as if chilled by an icy blast. A few headlines were just romanticising the relationship between herself and Javier. Some said they'd secretly dated for months, some claimed she'd seduced him on an aeroplane, others claimed they'd met by accident in Italy.

The same four pictures featured over and over again. How on earth had they got that picture on the private beach?

The boat. The boat moored in the distance. There must have been a photographer on board. She felt physically sick.

The picture at the restaurant or opera could have been taken by any of the other guests who'd recognised them. But the one on the balcony? She groaned. If they'd been recognised at the opera, it wouldn't have taken any reporter worth their salt long to figure out where they were staying. Years ago that reporter might have been her. That balcony looked over the whole bay. It was just that the picture was *so* close, *so* clear.

Her stomach lurched as she reached the next version of the headlines. There were video clips. She clicked on the first and her producer's face filled the screen. It was only a ten-second burst.

'Well, I told her she had three weeks to go and get a story and she certainly did that! We'll get the full exclusive when she returns from her break next week...'

But it was the next translated headline that stopped her breathing. *Ignored by the Billionaire*. She clicked and started to speed-read.

No.

There in the middle of the page was Aldo's name, followed by the fact that he'd phoned Javier—his old friend—pleading for help before he'd committed suicide.

It felt as if her blood had just turned to ice.

There was more. The reporter had tried to get comments from Aldo's family.

Oh, no. She glanced at when the report had appeared. It was only minutes ago in an Italian news website. It wouldn't take the US sites long to pick up the story and start to run with it. She knew how these things worked.

She grabbed the paper and ran out of the café. She had to find Javier. She had to warn him. She had to speak to him now.

Her chest was tight. She needed to find Javier.

But there was no sign of him around the port area and the more she looked, the more she got suspicious glances.

She flagged a taxi. She'd go back to Villa Rosa. It was safer there. Javier would appear eventually and she would have a chance to talk to him then.

But as soon as they pulled up outside the pale pink villa her stomach dropped. The front door was lying wide open.

She thrust some money at the taxi driver and rushed up the steps. 'Javier?' she shouted.

There was no reply. She ran up the stairs and headed for his room.

His room was in complete disarray. All his clothes were scattered across the bed, wardrobe still open and drawers askew. Javier's face was like thunder as he was blindly stuffing everything into his bag.

'Javier?' The air was almost black in the room. She was almost scared to speak.

The look he gave her almost cut her in two.

'Did you enjoy your story? Did I give you what you need? Do you know what's happened to Aldo's family in the last few hours? There are paparazzi camped outside their house—banging on their door and harassing them. How do you think they can deal with that?' He didn't even stop to draw breath, he just kept thundering on.

'I don't care that you used me, Portia. I don't care that all that you ever wanted was a headline to keep your job. Funny how you never mentioned that to me. But what I will never, *ever* forgive you for is the fact you used a grieving family to feather your own nest.'

The last item of clothing was stuffed in the bag. His face was red, his eyes blazing. She'd never, ever seen him like this.

'Wait, that's not what happened. I was going to tell you about my job—I was going to tell you that I was giving it up. That it wasn't for me any more. But I wanted to wait until I got back to LA and talked to my producer. I would never do something like this. Don't you know that?'

Javier grabbed his bag from the bed. 'What I do know, Portia, is that the woman I thought I knew doesn't exist at all. You knew, Portia, you knew what I experienced as a child. You knew how my mother was treated then. But you didn't care.

You just wanted your story.' He glanced up and down her body and shook his head. 'Boy, you're good. You had me believing that this might actually be real.'

She was stunned. She couldn't find the words to speak. It was her that had had all the fears. The fears that she might be played. The fears that Javier Russo might not really be interested in her.

She tried to speak but he lifted his hand in front of her face. 'Answer me one question: your boss, did she or did she not give you three weeks to find a story or you'd be fired?'

The words stuck at the back of her throat. She knew exactly how this would sound. Her heart was twisting in her chest. In less than an hour her life had turned upside down. The love that she'd never been sure she'd encounter was right in front of her but slipping from her grasp in a way she hadn't even imagined.

'Javier…' It came out as a croak and he shot her a look of disgust as he shouldered his way past her and thundered down the corridor.

For a second he paused, then he shook his head and disappeared down the stairs.

She wanted to slide right down the wall onto the floor. But she couldn't. She had to see this through. She had to fight for what she wanted and who she believed in. Her heart was crumpling in her chest. The guy she'd lain next to only the day before. The guy who could make her skin tingle just by looking at her. The man she'd actually dared to picture a future with. The man she loved with her whole heart and she hadn't even had the chance to tell him.

It couldn't end like this. It just couldn't.

She pushed herself back from the wall and started down the corridor. There was a noise outside and every part of her body clenched.

No. Her feet moved faster, down the stairs and across the hallway to the main door, which was still lying wide open.

She reached the door just in time to see the taxi pull out of the driveway onto the road back to the village. He'd jumped in the taxi she'd just left. She started to run, shouting at the taxi to stop. But either the driver didn't see her, or Javier told him to ignore her.

One glance at her watch told her everything she

needed to know. The next ferry left in ten minutes. The taxi would make it there just in time.

She—would not.

Her legs crumpled beneath her and she started to sob.

The job she used to love had just snatched away the life she was about to lead.

And she had no idea how to put it right.

CHAPTER NINE

NOTHING ABOUT THIS felt right. Everything about this felt wrong.

From the second he'd hit the mainland on his way to Naples airport his phone had pinged non-stop. His friends, relatives, newspaper reporters, showbiz contacts, acting contemporaries and… his agent.

He only replied to one message from Aldo's sister. His reply was simple.

On my way.

He had the luxury of being rushed through security and boarding the private jet he'd hired in under an hour.

But from the second the plane took off he had only one thing on his mind.

Portia.

When he'd seen the newspaper he'd been shocked. The pictures were intrusive. But they also made him feel like a fool. Over the last few years he'd got used to people snapping photos wherever he went. It seemed that every person in the world these days had a phone in their hand.

But L'Isola dei Fiori had felt different. He'd been more relaxed, let his guard down, and in doing so he'd inadvertently exposed Portia to something she might not have wanted to make front-page news with.

Or so he'd thought.

When one of the shopkeepers had gestured him in to look at his computer and watch the video clip of Portia's producer he'd felt physically sick. But more than that he'd felt betrayed.

He'd always been wary of reporters but he'd never contemplated the fact their relationship was contrived or false. It had never entered his head—the connection had just seemed so real. He felt like such a fool. She'd hardly mentioned work at all—and when she had she'd been a little evasive. Now he knew why. He'd trusted her with a secret that had kept him awake at night for the last few months and she'd revealed it to the world.

He'd known not to trust reporters. He'd known to keep them always at arm's length. To control how he appeared, and what he revealed.

But around Portia? His walls had been chipped away, until they'd finally tumbled down.

He'd trusted her. Trust wasn't something that came easily to Javier. And she'd betrayed him—just when he'd thought about taking their relationship to the next level.

He'd finally come to terms with how to move forward. And it had felt good. It had felt as if he could actually do something that might make a difference.

And it was freeing. Because he'd been able to recognise how he actually felt about Portia.

He loved her. Her English accent. Her dark brown eyes. The way she said his name. The way her clothes hugged her curves, and the way her smile could reach from ear to ear.

He was just glad he hadn't been fool enough to tell her.

That would have been an even bigger disaster than the one he faced now.

He absolutely didn't care what the newspapers and social media said about him.

What he cared about was the impact on Aldo's family. That was his priority. They were the people he had to sit down with, look in the eye and tell the truth to.

This was never the way he'd wanted this to happen.

He was trying to ignore the fact his heart felt as if it had been speared clean from his chest. He was trying to ignore the fact that he still couldn't really believe what had gone around about him.

His phone beeped. His agent and publicist were having a meltdown.

It seemed now that Portia's temporary replacement on Entertainment Buzz TV was being very uncomplimentary about her. Some of his fellow celebs were commenting on what a good match Javier and Portia were, and how they looked so happy together.

He was getting interview requests by the second.

His phone beeped again. This time it was the

head of the film company for the action movie he was due to start promoting. The message was short and to the point.

Good work.

The irony made him shake his head. David McCurrie always said that all publicity was good publicity. Javier hitting the headlines a few weeks before the film premiere would be right up his street.

His heart weighed heavily in his chest. The betrayal was the hardest sting. He'd let Portia get under his guard. He'd believed what she'd said.

He closed his eyes for a second and leaned back against the leather seat. Yesterday he'd been planning out his whole life in his head. A whole life that included Portia.

Today, he just felt empty. Empty, sad and betrayed.

The more he thought about those photos, the more confused he felt. There had been no one on the beach. He had no idea how someone had got the photo on the balcony in Naples. How sensible had it really been to walk out on a balcony overlooking the Bay of Naples? Was there really no privacy anywhere in the world?

But the thing that annoyed him most of all was still the news about Aldo's phone call. The only person he'd ever told about that was Portia. She was the only person that knew Aldo had told him he really needed to talk. Guilt washed over him again.

And now that was front-page news.

Was he really such a poor judge of character? Every cell in his body told him Portia would never do something like that. But it was front-page news. Along with the fact that she'd been given a deadline to find a story.

It didn't matter how he looked at it—in every version of this story, Javier Russo had been played.

CHAPTER TEN

GETTING A FLIGHT home from Italy was tougher than she'd thought. As soon as she'd hit the mainland her phone had pinged non-stop.

It was her sisters. It seemed it didn't matter where they were in the world—they'd seen the headlines too.

Naples airport was busy. And Portia was now in the unfortunate position of being recognised. Thank goodness her Italian was awful. She had no idea what the few reporters that were there were saying to her, and the girl at the check-in desk gave her a gracious nod, upgraded her and swept her up to the private lounge.

Portia was embarrassed. 'I'm not really famous,' she muttered.

The girl turned towards her—her English impeccable. 'No, but you're being harassed by the press and I won't leave you with those vultures.'

Those few words had been enough to let the tears that were brimming beneath the surface come flooding out. She'd been ushered into the lounge, then onto the plane. Eighteen hours later, after a touchdown in Munich, she finally arrived in Los Angeles.

She hadn't slept. Once she'd picked herself up from the driveway of Villa Rosa she'd contemplated opening a bottle of wine and losing herself in it.

Instead, a fire had burned inside her and she'd started to plot.

She'd emailed her boss. It had taken less than a minute to send her 'I quit' email. The press of a button had never felt so good.

LAX was notorious for paparazzi—but Portia had insider information. She knew a way to duck out avoiding most of the places the press would be waiting. At least her job had been good for something.

Her empty apartment had a stillness about it she wasn't ready for. She dumped her bag at the door and crossed the floor of her lounge. Her footsteps echoed on the wooden floor. A sob caught in her throat. She looked around.

She'd always loved this place. Loved being in the heart of Hollywood and only a short walk from Griffith Park. But all of a sudden it felt like a million miles from everyone and everything she loved.

Most of her friends were connected with work.

Her family seemed like a lifetime away.

She'd quit her job. She probably had enough savings to pay the next four or five months' rent and then she'd be out.

Her phone beeped again and she lifted it up. Immi.

Portia sagged down onto the sofa. She was sure something was going on with her sister—the last thing Immi needed was to listen to Portia's problems. But it was almost as if her sister had a sixth sense. As soon as the pictures had hit the press she'd kept texting, asking Portia to get in touch.

And it wasn't high-five texts like those she'd got from some Hollywood friends. Immi wasn't dazzled by the thought of her sister dating a film star.

Portia took a deep breath and pressed 'Call'.

Immi answered instantly. 'Tell me you're okay.'

It didn't matter that Immi sounded anxious; for Portia the familiarity of her voice was like a snuggly blanket. Comfort. That was what she needed right now.

'Tell me *you're* okay,' she replied quickly. 'Is something going on? I feel as if there's something you aren't telling me.'

There was a long sigh at the end of the phone. 'Deflection, deflection, deflection, Portia. And it isn't going to work. To answer your questions, I'm fine. We can talk about me later. Just know that I have everything under control. Now, tell me what's *really* going on.'

A tear snaked down Portia's cheek. She was so used to being the big sister. She was so used to being the one that had stuck plasters on her sisters' knees and stopped their squabbles.

'Portia? Are you crying? Talk to me. Tell me about Javier Russo. I don't need to ask what you've been doing because I've seen it. But I want to know how you are. I want to know what's happened.'

Portia licked her dry lips. Her case was still bulging by the door. She had half a mind to pick it straight back up and find another flight to somewhere else in the world.

Immi kept talking. 'I know he was in Italy this morning. I know he visited the family of the friend people are talking about. And if I believe what I hear on the news, he's currently on his way back to LA.'

Portia's heart nearly stopped. Javier was coming back here? Why? What for?

'Portia. Talk to me now. If you don't start talking I'm going to climb on a plane and shake you until you do.'

The words stuck part way in her throat. 'I…I don't know what to say…'

It was clear Immi was getting exasperated. 'Well, say something!'

The tears just started to flow. 'I've made such a mess of things. I've quit my job—'

'What?'

'And Javier thinks I've betrayed him. He thinks I lied to him. He thinks I broke the story about what happened with his friend. I would never do that. Never.'

'Well, of course you wouldn't. And why on earth would he think that?'

Portia sniffed. 'Because he hadn't told anyone else. Just me. Next thing it was plastered all over the news. He thinks it was me.'

She could hear the change in Immi's voice. 'What kind of a man is this Javier Russo? Doesn't he know you at all?'

Portia's voice broke. 'But I hadn't told him. I hadn't told him that my boss had given me an ultimatum to find a story.'

Immi's voice softened. 'Why not?'

'Because I didn't want him to think badly of me. He hated the press. They harassed his mother when he was a young boy. He didn't trust anyone in the press.'

'But he must have trusted you. I'm assuming from the way you were wrapped around him you got up close and personal?' Portia closed her eyes. She could picture Immi right now with her eyebrows arched as she asked the question.

She sagged a little further on the sofa. 'Yes.'

'And now—you've fought?'

'Yes.' It was all she could get out.

'Tell me what you think of him. Tell me what you really think of Javier Russo. And no holding back. Is this man really worth your tears? He's a film star, after all—aren't they all just smoke and mirrors?'

Portia blinked back her tears. It was a reasonable question. She'd moaned often enough to her sisters about the lies and betrayals in Hollywood.

She squeezed her eyes shut again and took a deep breath. 'I know that the man I met on L'Isola dei Fiori has the biggest heart on the planet. He's nothing like the arrogant man I've met on the red carpet. Most people watch Javier on a movie screen and just see the sexy Italian star with a twinkle in his eye. There's so much more to him than that. He's caring. He's hard-working. He wants to do his absolute best. I was lucky to spend time with him. I was lucky to connect with him in a way I've never connected with anyone before. He made me feel confident. He made me feel sure. He made me want to do better in this life.' She couldn't believe she'd actually just said all that out loud.

'Oh, no.'

'What do you mean—oh, no?'

Immi spoke in a voice that sounded so much older than her years. 'I mean, oh, no. You've fallen for him. You're in love. You never speak like this about anyone. Never. He's broken your heart—hasn't he? Right, that's it. Get me an address. Javier Russo is going to meet the Marlowe sisters in a way he could never even imagine.'

Portia choked out a laugh. She could only imagine her sisters stampeding Javier and letting him witness the full extent of the Marlowe sisters' ire.

She shook her head. 'Stop it, Immi. You can't do that. I don't know his address.' Those words made her heart squeeze. She hadn't asked Javier for his address. They hadn't got around to it.

'Why?' asked Immi, her voice wavering slightly. 'You'd do the same for me.' Her voice softened. 'What else are sisters for?'

Portia smiled. She wiped away her tears. 'Thank you, honey. It's good to talk. I need to take some time to decide what to do next.'

Immi was quiet for a second. 'Okay. You'll call me if you need me?'

'Only if you call me if you need me.' Immi gave a little sigh. 'Let's talk in a few days.'

'Done.'

Portia rang off, pushed herself off the sofa and walked over to the window. Hollywood wasn't for her any more. Not like this.

But there was some place she still wanted to go.

CHAPTER ELEVEN

HIS PHONE STARTED buzzing as soon as he landed. Text after text after text.

His visit with Aldo's parents and sister had been short and sweet. Aldo's mother and father were upset by the press intrusion but the local *polizia* had moved them on. They'd known Aldo's last call had been to Javier. They'd known Javier hadn't got it. They hadn't known about the message.

But they'd handled it well. They didn't blame Javier. They knew he'd been filming in the middle of nowhere and working long hours. They'd been heartened by the news of his plans for the charity and the helpline. Their reaction had given him new vigour.

The paparazzi were waiting at the airport. Swarming around him. A private security firm kept them at a distance as their cameras snapped and their shouted questions all just merged into noise.

A car was waiting for him. He climbed into the back and leaned back against the cool leather seats. He was tired. He hadn't slept at all.

He ignored the texts and the messages on his phone, instead pulling up his browser, his fingers poised over the keys. He knew better than to do this. He did. But his fingers worked automatically.

The first hit surprised him.

Holly Payne lands Entertainment Buzz TV's top job after Portia Marlowe quits.

It was only a few hours old.

He straightened up in the seat. Why would Portia quit?

The horrible nagging feeling that had been in his stomach since he'd left Villa Rosa intensified.

His mind started to swirl. Portia had quit. That wasn't the sign of someone chasing a story. That wasn't the actions of a woman that was trying to entice someone into revealing details of their life.

He groaned and ran his fingers through his

hair. It didn't matter that the car was air-conditioned, sweat started to break out on his skin.

He searched on his phone. There. A picture of the journalist that had broken the story. An Italian journalist. His mouth was dry. He recognised the guy.

The man from the next balcony in the hotel in Naples.

He'd heard every word.

Every part of Javier's body cringed. It was obviously intentional. The man had deliberately booked into the next suite to his. Hoping to find a story. And he'd got it.

He could feel his heart thud against his chest. Everything he'd hoped. All the plans he'd had in his head. Plans for him and Portia.

He groaned. He should have trusted her. He should have stopped to think. It didn't matter that he hadn't told anyone else—there was always a chance that an investigative reporter could dig deep. Celebrities' phones had been bugged before. Messages had been listened to. He should have realised. He should have thought a little harder about the glimpse on the balcony.

A trickle of sweat ran down his back. He had to speak to Portia. He had to find her.

He looked around. Hollywood. He hadn't even asked her where she lived. He had no idea where she might be.

Had she even left Villa Rosa—might she still be there?

The skyline changed in front of him and something came into view. Something that made his heart twist. His reaction was automatic.

He leaned forward and touched the driver's shoulder. 'Change of plan.'

The driver turned his head slightly. 'Mr Russo?'

'Take me to Griffith Park.'

The wind was whipping up a storm. When she'd changed and dashed outside she hadn't thought to bring a jacket. It was almost ironic. The outfit she'd grabbed from her case to put on was the pink satin dress she'd worn with Javier.

Normally when she came to the observatory she wore jeans, a T-shirt and running shoes. Today, she had the running shoes along with a satin dress. She'd already had a few odd stares. But she didn't care.

From here she could look out over LA. She could see the city beneath her.

Part of her loved it and part of her was tired of it. She just had to decide what to do next.

She'd been up here for hours. Her hair was tangled in knots with the wind and she was definitely feeling the chill. The crowds had thinned too. A lot of the tourists had vanished for the day. If she waited much longer, the place would be full of teenagers searching for a quiet corner. Nothing like young love to make you feel old. And broken-hearted. And useless.

She brushed her feet on the ground in front of her. It was time to move on. Time to make a change. Maybe she could finish that book? Maybe taking a complete break might do her some good. Help her re-evaluate. Help her decide what she wanted to do with her life.

Her eyes squinted in front of her. There was something familiar about the figure striding towards her.

She put her hands up to shade her eyes as he

neared. There was a pitter-patter in her chest. She wasn't imagining things. She wasn't dreaming. The guy in the jeans and T-shirt really was who she thought it was.

Javier? Here?

His steps slowed as he neared and he pushed his sunglasses up on his head.

The steady grey eyes made her suck in her breath. 'Hi,' he said quickly, before he looked downwards and gave her a smile. 'Nice shoes.'

For a second she was stuck for words. Last time she'd seen him he'd yelled at her. Accused her of lying. Accused her of playing him.

She glanced around to check she wasn't hallucinating. Nope. That was definitely Javier Russo standing in front of her.

Her heart did that silly pitter-patter again. She wasn't usually lost for words. This just seemed surreal. Javier Russo at Griffith Park. The place she'd told him she loved the most in LA.

She glanced down at her red running shoes and wiggled her feet. 'Yeah, I think so. Come in handy around about here.' She pressed her lips together for a second. She couldn't help the next words that came out of her mouth. 'How are Aldo's family? Are they okay?'

Javier sighed and sat down next to her, taking off his sunglasses and turning them over in his hands. 'Yeah, they are. They aren't angry at me. They say they understand.'

He looked out across the skyline. There were lines around his eyes. He looked exhausted.

'You don't believe them?' she asked.

He shook his head. 'I do.' His head dipped for a few moments and he leaned forward with his elbows on his knees.

Portia nodded. 'I hope they're going to be okay.'

Javier looked straight back at her with those sincere grey eyes. 'But will we?'

It was as if something had struck her in the chest. It just seemed to cannonball out of nowhere. For a few moments there she'd thought they might tiptoe around each other for a bit. But it seemed that Javier had decided to go straight to the heart of the matter.

She followed his lead. 'Is there a "we"?'

Right now, she couldn't suck in a breath. A million thoughts were flying through her head. Not a single one of them made any sense. An imaginary fist felt as if it were clamped around her heart. She didn't want to believe that this could actually be real. He was actually here with her now.

He turned towards her, pulling one leg up on the bench seat so his chest was entirely facing her. They were in the middle of one of the most popular tourist destinations in LA. No one had noticed them. No one had commented.

She hadn't pretended when she'd said this was her favourite place and something about this felt so right. Whatever was going to happen to her life in LA, it seemed fitting that it should happen here. Javier reached towards her, his fingers stopping a few millimetres from her cheek. 'I never told you something.'

All the little hairs on her body stood on end. It wasn't the wind. It wasn't the temperature. It was every cell in her body preparing itself for what could come next. She tried to keep her voice steady. 'What didn't you tell me?'

His finger moved forward and brushed against

her cheek. 'I never told you that in the last few weeks I discovered something about myself.'

'What was that?'

He met her gaze. 'I found out I'd met my soul mate. I met someone who made me happy. Who supported me. Who challenged me. Someone I could picture myself growing old with.'

Portia's heart thudded against her chest as he kept talking. 'Fate had put her in my path before, but it wasn't until I got to Villa Rosa that I understood why. I'm sorry, Portia. I'm so, so sorry. I couldn't think straight. I was so worried about Aldo's family.'

She shook her head, her voice shaking. 'Javier, you thought I'd betrayed your trust. You didn't even give me a chance to explain—not that I knew what the explanation was at the time. But you just upped and left. Is that how you treat your soul mate? Do you know what that did to me?' Tears were brimming in her eyes.

'I'm sorry, Portia. I was stupid. I was selfish. From the moment I left your side, you've been in my head. Nothing about this felt right. I jumped to a stupid conclusion. I know it wasn't you. It was the guy on the balcony next to us in Naples.' He shook his head. 'But I should have let you explain. I let my past experience with the press cloud my judgement. I've spent my life trying to protect myself, only revealing what I wanted to the rest of the world. The truth is I've never connected with someone the way I've connected with you. I am *so* sorry. So, so sorry I didn't take the time to stop and think. To believe in the person that I know you are—and always will be.'

The tears started to flow. 'And I felt the same. But you didn't trust me. You didn't give me a chance to explain. You walked away, Javier.' She shook her head. 'Do you know how much that hurt?'

He reached up and touched her cheek. 'And I'm so, so sorry. Portia, I went to Villa Rosa looking for peace. Looking for a place to regroup, and get my life back to a way I wanted it to be. And then…' he paused and smiled '…I found you. The crazy, unwelcoming Englishwoman who assaulted me and accused me of breaking in.'

The memories flooded back through her. 'You took me by surprise.'

'You took me by surprise too.' He ran his fingers through her tangled hair. 'And not just down on the beach.' He pulled her forward and rested his forehead against hers. 'I never expected to go to Villa Rosa and find love,' he whispered. 'I wasn't ready for it. And I didn't recognise it right away.'

She gave a little wheeze, her words caught in her throat.

'But for the first time in my life I've found a real connection. Someone I want to talk to, to share with—to fight with. Someone who can challenge me, and match me in every way. Someone I want to wake up with. And that's you, Portia. Every single day.'

A tear slid down her cheek as she pulled her head back and tilted her chin up towards him. 'I felt that way too. I stopped thinking about you as Javier Russo the film star. You were just Javier to me. The guy that wanted to help others. The guy that had a bigger heart than I could ever have imagined. The guy that stole my own heart away.'

His face broke into a smile. 'I stole your heart?'

She raised her eyebrows. 'You trampled it.' She

shook her head. 'You don't get to do that again. You don't get to not talk to me. You don't get to walk away.'

He gave a slow nod. 'I promise.'

But she shook her head. 'Hollywood is full of promises. None of them I believe.'

He raised one eyebrow. 'The woman who doesn't believe in love.' He tilted his head a little. 'But you told me I stole your heart.'

'But can I trust you with it?'

It was bold. It was brash. But they'd come too far.

Javier didn't hesitate. He knelt down in front of her. 'You've quit your job?'

She nodded, wondering where this was going. 'Yes.'

'Have you found another one?'

She gave a little smile. 'Not yet. I may be considering other career plans.'

He took her hands in his. 'I want us to be together. Not just for now. Forever. What do you think, Portia? I love you. I want to find a way for us to plan for a future. Do you think we can find a way to stay together in this crazy world?'

Something surged inside her. She wanted to wrap her hands around his neck and cry with relief. But she wouldn't. She wouldn't let herself.

She straightened her back and looked him in the eye. 'So what comes next?'

'Whatever you want.'

She licked her lips. She wasn't going to tell him what she wanted even though she knew deep down in her heart. 'What do you want to do?'

He nodded slowly and pulled her up into his arms. 'I have three houses. Pick one. We can stay anywhere you want.'

'And?'

'And, I want to hire a plane. I want to take you back to Italy and introduce you to the Lake Como house first. But before that, we have something else to do.'

'What's that?'

He bent down and kissed her. 'I've wasted enough time. When you know, you just know.' He placed his hand over his heart. 'And believe me, Portia, I know. There's something that we need before we get to Lake Como. It's just a formality. Do you have your passport and birth certificate?'

Her heart surged in her chest. She almost thought she knew what he was hinting at. 'Yes, but why?'

He grinned. 'Then let's go to the Italian consulate before we get on the plane.' He swept her up into his arms and she let out a squeal. 'Hey, I'm doing things early.'

He leaned his forehead against hers. 'How about I promise to carry you over the threshold in Lake Como too?'

She smiled as she wound her arms around his neck. 'What about the Hollywood house and the Malibu beach house?'

'Mrs Russo,' he whispered, 'are you always going to be this demanding?'

She kissed him on the lips. 'Oh, believe me, Mr Russo, I'm only just getting started. Hold on for the ride!'

EPILOGUE

He wasn't nervous at all. The paperwork was completed, the minister in place, the garden decorated and the families placated.

He'd surprised Portia with a huge engagement ring that she'd worn for five days. But Portia had assured him she was only interested in the thin rose-gold wedding band they'd picked together.

At the bottom of the garden, looking out over Lake Como, the florist had created their own Neptune's arch made entirely of pink and white flowers.

Portia was an uncomplicated bride. She didn't want fuss. She didn't want a million arrangements and the hint of press anywhere near them. She'd picked a dress from a local wedding shop that fitted perfectly and could be bought immediately. Pink flowers were threaded through her hair and in her bouquet. Her traditional wedding dress was cinched with a pink satin sash similar to the dress she'd been wearing a few days ago. Her dark hair tumbled about her shoulders and her eyes shone.

It was a simple civil ceremony with a blessing from the minister of the local church and two witnesses pulled from the luxury villa next door.

Portia's brown eyes brimmed with tears as they said their vows. He'd never seen a bride look more beautiful. 'For better or for worse, in sickness and in health, for as long as we both shall live,' she repeated, sincerity emanating from every pore in her body. Then she smiled and added a few lines of her own. 'I never found anyone that made me feel complete, made me feel whole, until I met you, Javier. I promise to love you, respect you and challenge you, every single day for the rest of your life.'

He couldn't wipe the smile from his face. He repeated the vows looking into the face of the woman that he loved. When he finished he kept hold of her hands. 'Portia Russo.' He gave a little laugh. 'I'm going to love saying those words.' He shook his head. 'When I went to Villa Rosa

I didn't expect to meet anyone. I wasn't ready to meet anyone. But then there was you. All English accent, twinkling eyes and very, very long legs. You made me smile, you made me laugh. You asked all the right questions. And before I knew it, I was in love. Hook, line and sinker. Don't ever let me go. Because I plan on us growing very old together.'

He bent to kiss her, her perfect lips on his, and then she wrapped her arms around his neck and whispered in his ear, 'I guess we should make this official.'

He swept her up into his arms, ready to carry her over the threshold of their home. 'It will be my pleasure, Mrs Russo.'

* * * * *

If you've loved this book then make sure you read CHRISTMAS IN THE BOSS'S CASTLE by Scarlet Wilson, part of MAIDS UNDER THE MISTLETOE. *Available now!*

If you loved this story, and want to indulge in the next Mediterranean romance in the SUMMER AT VILLA ROSA *quartet, the third book, THE RUNAWAY BRIDE AND THE BILLIONAIRE by Kate Hardy, is out next month!*